One Thing *At A* Time

DEBORAH McVAY-McKINNEY

InspiringVoices®

Inspiring Voices books may be ordered through booksellers or by contacting:

Inspiring Voices
1663 Liberty Drive
Bloomington, IN 47403
www.inspiringvoices.com
844-686-9605

ISBN: 978-1-4624-1312-6 (sc)
ISBN: 978-1-4624-1313-3 (e)

Library of Congress Control Number: 2020918500

Print information available on the last page.

Inspiring Voices rev. date: 10/29/2020

For all the Esthers of our time,

especially mine.

CONTENTS

ACKNOWLEDGEMENTS

This book would not be possible without all the people who have given their love and support to me for as long as I can remember and who I can never thank enough:

- My baby girl who fills my life with fun, joy, and laughter.
- My grown-up girl who gives me the complete honor of being her other mom.
- A family who has loved me through more ups and downs than I can count, year after year. I don't know how I would have made it this far without you.
- Each and every BFF – so, so many who I could never do this life without.
- And my love, who makes every step in this journey worth taking.

What a blessing from God to live this life with each of you.

AUTHOR'S FORWARD

Tell your story. Write your story. You have a good one, you know. Just talk from your heart.

People have been saying these things to me for a long time. So I finally decided to do that. I'm going to tell you the story of a great life that fell completely apart and became an awful life. And how bit by bit and with one thing at a time, a life in a deep pit of despair turned into a life full of more blessings than imaginable.

Why does it matter? Because each of us has a story that needs to be told. Because what I've learned from listening to others talk about their often crazy and sometimes lives full of just plain bad choices is that everyone has something in their past that they wish they would not have done. And if you stick with this story, you may feel sad, shake your head and ask why, or maybe get angry. But in the end, my wish is for you to feel the joy that I have come to know from the lessons learned. To discern the God whispers we should all follow. To know when you take a genuine, all in leap of faith, life can be turned into one so amazing there is no way you ever could have planned it to turn out that way.

It's funny that I always wanted to write the great American novel. A love story with characters you wanted to know, be your friends, relatives, or next door neighbors. Instead, I wrote my first book, telling busy women how to find some balance and peace in their lives. It was really meant as a tribute to my mother and grandmother, who taught me the value of being organized. They had both passed away six weeks to the day of each other ten years ago; the same year I celebrated a milestone birthday and wondered if I was ever going to reach my life-long goal of publishing a book. It was actually a call of encouragement I received just over a year later from my stepmother that gave me the push I needed to finally get started. She called one day and asked me, "Are you ever going to write your book? There's a writing contest you should enter if you are." So, I thought, 'why not?' Fortunately, I had a lot of notes from speaking about the things I wanted to cover in my book, so it was easy to start. It's the finishing that's the difficult part.

Have you ever wanted to write and publish a book? I quickly learned why people either write or they go to work elsewhere. Writing truly is a full-time job. Not only do you need something to say, and something that might interest other people enough to read it, but you have to write it in a way that makes logical sense. Then it needs edited by a third party which can be very costly. Fortunately, I have a dear friend with this ability who offered to be my editor. And he dropped everything to edit my story in time for me to enter that contest. So, off the third revision went to the contest. Of course I didn't win! But, the publisher reached out and asked if I wanted to publish it anyway. Well, I had come this far, so why not?

"Ok," I said. Done! Not exactly. Next came a series of decisions: What do you want the cover to look like? Send us a picture of yourself and describe yourself in 50 words or less (no pressure there). Use 75 words to describe the highlights of your story. What color do you want the paper to be? What font? What type of spacing? Oh my goodness! OK, got that done.

Then the day came when the package arrived in the mail. You know the packaging of the corrugated cardboard envelope that sticks together around the outside edges and contains a book you can't wait to begin reading? This time the one that arrived addressed to me contained my final product. Mine! Wow!

So, with shaking hands, I opened the envelope and pulled out my very own published book! What do you think that feels like? It's difficult to describe. I stood in my kitchen and just stared at it. Then I started thinking, who cares what I have to say? Does any of this make sense? Does it matter?

My answer is that it doesn't matter at all. If this is your goal, go for it!

Fortunately, I have an amazing support system of family, friends, neighbors, clients, community, and more who actually bought the book. Several local publications wrote about the book and it was picked up by other publications across the country. Granted it never became a million copy best seller, but people were very nice to let me know they enjoyed it. (And I know they read it because they told me about parts of it that touched home for them.) So again, if this is your goal, just do it! You won't be sorry.

Since I published that first book, people have come and gone in my life. I always wanted to tell another type of story. One that would give hope and inspiration long after the reader finished it and set it aside. The story I am about to tell you is the one I've been trying to tell for a long time. It comes from a place in my heart that has been visited by many people I've known along the way. Their stories combined to make up two very special people you will read about here.

I trust you will hold them in your heart and love them as I do.

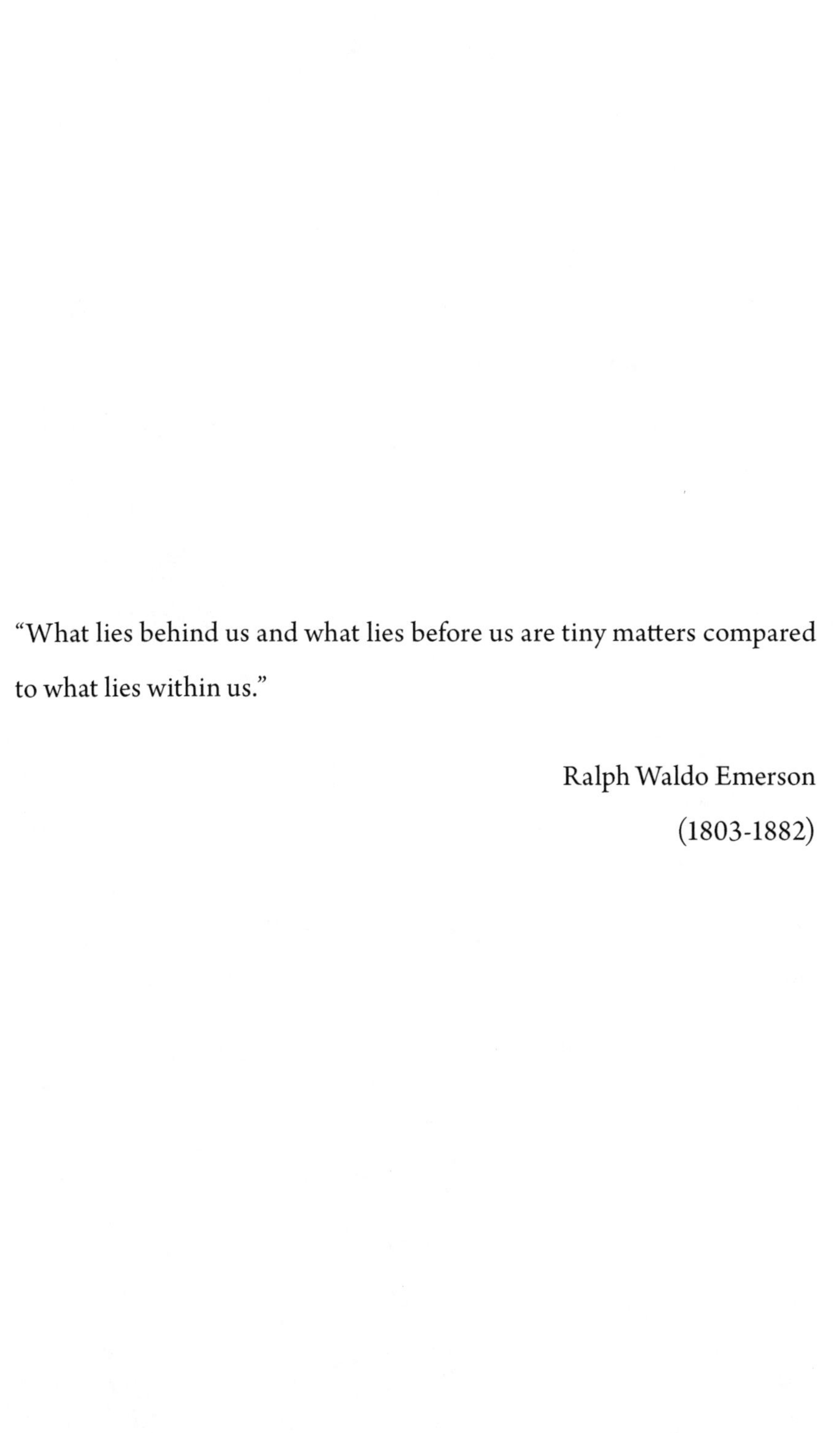

"What lies behind us and what lies before us are tiny matters compared to what lies within us."

Ralph Waldo Emerson

(1803-1882)

Chapter One

Tell Your Story

As with all stories, I think the best place to start is at the beginning. And to tell the truth, my own story is not that interesting when it comes right down to it. So instead, I'm going to tell you the story of someone I knew some years ago. Her name was Carolee and she had quite the story to tell. My hope is that it gives you the courage to tell your own.

Carolee was from a forgotten time. Back when there were no cell phones, or cable TV stations, or microwave ovens. She was born at the end of the baby boomer era and before the women's rights movement came to be.

On the surface it appeared she came from the all-American family. She had a mom and a dad and two brothers; she was the middle child. Each had their own unique personality, but together never quite seemed to fit together - except to the outside world.

I met Carolee just a few years ago but she was one of those people you felt like you had known your whole life. She was a talker for sure! But what she talked about was her past and how she had found that through faith anything - everything – actually is possible. She was very open about her story but never believed it was one anybody would care to know. Just so you know, as she talked and I listened and she started remembering more, I knew I had to ask her if I could tell her story. Carolee hesitantly gave me permission, but she really didn't think it was interesting at all. But, if you keep reading, I think you'll agree with me that it is definitely a story worth knowing.

The first thing Carolee did was ask me, "What's your very first memory in life?" She suggested I stop a second and try to remember. Carolee continued, "Personally, I have blurry ideas and sometimes I wonder if they are because I've seen pictures, or are they from a dream, or do I actually remember?"

This is Carolee's story.

I was born in New York City, since my parents were working artists there; my mother a designer and my father a photographer. When I was just four months old, my mother had an opportunity to showcase her designs in Europe, so off went our little family of four. Funny that I have never had any desire to return to Europe or even outside the United States. Maybe because I have no memory at all from this time in my early life. Although, I do have a photo of our family sitting under a tree enjoying a picnic somewhere that looks like a scene from an old black and white movie.

Anyway, I vaguely remember scenes from life as a toddler back in the United States when we moved to the New England coast a couple of years later. One of my memories is me sitting in a highchair wearing a party hat. It must have been my third birthday. I got a southern belle doll that sat contained under a plastic dome, which I kept all through junior high school. She didn't leave that dome until I was in third or fourth grade and I wanted to touch her silk dress all fanned out underneath her.

I also remember swinging on a swing set in our backyard when my older brother Jim suddenly fell backwards into the chain link fence. I have a vision of holding his head and my hand being covered in blood, all the while crying because I thought my hand was bleeding!

The next winter, my brother and I were playing in the snow when my parents came outside and got in their car. Once again, I remember crying for my mother but a neighbor lady shushed me, saying, "Your mommy is going to the hospital to bring home your new brother or sister."

When I was five, I was in a car accident in my parent's old Volkswagen bus during an awful rainstorm when my mother was driving. To this day, I remember standing on the floor in the backseat with a couple of other little girls and my mother telling me to sit down. Then, I remember hitting my face against the back of the driver's seat and once again crying out.

I think at this point Carolee realized what she had just shared. She stopped and asked me, "Maybe we only remember the traumatic times?" I replied, "I'm not sure. But, I heard a quote once – I can't remember where: *The past only has the power you give it.*"

Tilting her head to one side, she responded, "That's very true. Well, anyway," she continued...

Once we went to someone's home for dinner and my plate had a huge helping of lima beans on it. I do not like lima beans to this day and I still remember saying then, "I don't like lima beans!" But I also clearly remember my dad telling me to eat them and not be rude. You see, we were raised in a very Victorian manner where children are to be seen and not heard. Children are to be polite at all times. And children are never to be disrespectful to elders. Ever! Rules that make me very proud of who I am today but were very difficult to understand as a child. That dinner was one of my first memories of an elegantly long dining table set with a pretty white linen cloth and flower arrangements. I'm not sure where we were, but the host had a cute dog. After dinner, we went out to the beach to play in the water with the dog.

My very last memory of Bridgeport was of my mother packing us three children in the station wagon and driving all through the night. I was five years old and our family was moving back to Ohio where my parents had been born and raised. We were going to live near my mother's parents in Columbus, the state capital, where they had recently moved. I learned later as a teenager the reason we moved was because the world was rapidly changing due to the on-going conflict in Vietnam. My dad, being a husband and father of three young children, knew it was time to do something more sustainable with his life.

So, off we moved to Ohio and into a tiny two-bedroom apartment. My mother went to work as a seamstress and my Dad returned to college to earn his second degree in business. To this day, some of my fondest memories are times spent with my maternal grandparents all through the rest of my life.

I don't have too many memories of that place except a dog chasing me home from school one day. Probably the same reason why I've never had any interest in owning a dog my entire life. I also remember going to a neighbor's house to watch *The Big Valley* on Monday nights in the first grade, while my mom and Jim stayed home to watch *Star Trek*. I love the old west, but never did get into outer space shows.

One time, my dad took the three of us children to a little town in eastern Ohio to buy new dishes for my mom. Little did I know it was a secret and when we got home, I ran in the door yelling, "Mommy, we got you new dishes!" It was supposed to be a Mother's Day surprise. Never one to keep secrets as a child, I did it again when I was in fifth grade! By that point, we had moved to a new neighborhood – one of those developments of cul-de-sacs and winding roads built on an old farm field with an elementary school at the end of the street. My dad was a Boy Scout leader and I had gone to JC Penney with my mom to buy him a new uniform. We came home and I ran inside to promptly report, "Daddy, we got you a Boy Scout uniform!" Well, that was supposed to be a Father's Day gift! (I eventually did learn from these lessons the importance of keeping a secret!)

Carolee paused. "Maybe I should tell you more about my mom and dad."

My parents met when they were young and graduated high school together. Once they went off to separate colleges, they reconnected within a couple of years and married. Three years later, my brother, Jim came along, followed 23 months later by me. When I was four, my younger brother Robert joined the family. I always wondered why my parents married, as they seemed to be complete opposites. Funny how love works. I think they did love each other deeply, but had a hard time being together. But, there were good times as I was growing up. And, we looked like the typical American happy family of five.

The street I lived on from second grade all the way through high school was a typical middle class one. One of my treasured friends to this day lived right next door. We had a former Miss Oklahoma and her philandering husband on the other side, the town mechanic and his family of hellions beside them, a quiet family of four next, an older childless couple beside them, I'm pretty sure some sort of criminals lived on the other side of them, and a former sports star, his blonde wife and adorable baby living on the end.

Carolee winked and with a grin shared, "It made for a complete soap opera."

Especially when the hellions would sneak out of their bedroom windows to cause havoc like setting their parent's car on fire in the driveway! Or the time the quiet family of four was confronted in the driveway by a wife from the next street over, demanding that the husband come out immediately and admit to his wife of their love affair! The police cruisers arrived many nights with lights flashing across the street and we never quite knew what was going on there. And the next door neighbor would race up the street in his convertible Stingray while his bombshell wife sunned herself in a string bikini in the backyard, much to the delight of all the husbands hanging over their fences to watch!

But, it was a great place to grow up.

We had so much fun in the summer. All the neighborhood kids rode our bikes for hours in the farm fields just beyond our neighborhood. We stopped to pick apples when we got hungry and took breaks to spin in circles and lay in the grass pointing out shapes from the clouds rolling by overhead. We tried to out whistle each other with thick blades of grass. We fashioned lemonade stands from old washing machine boxes and put playing cards in our bicycle wheels. There were potlucks and a makeshift parade on the Fourth of July. My brothers and I climbed out my bedroom window and sat on the garage roof of our traditional colonial home to watch the fireworks. We caught lightening bugs in jars and tried to feed them grass. Our parents would give us a penny for every beetle we plucked off the rose bushes and into a can of turpentine. We had a swimming pool in our backyard, so we all played in the water until our hands were shriveled.

Our elementary school offered summer camps each year. Even though all school year, we counted down the days till summer vacation, we would still walk the quarter mile to the school playground on hot humid days where we climbed trees, made plastic cord keychains, solved word search puzzles, drank Kool-Aid and ate cookies. We played cowboys and Indians, kings and queens, and other imaginary characters together. I don't ever remember an adult in sight, but I'm sure there were. When the Ohio State Fair came to town, we all piled into family station wagons and carpooled to the opening gates. It was truly the end of summer when we left at dark with sticky cotton candy and caramel apple hands.

At Halloween, we went trick or treating with pillowcases and came home to trade our sorted candy late into the night by flashlight, even though it was usually a school night and the three of us were long ago supposed to have been asleep. In the winter, we built forts and igloos out of snow drifts, had snowball fights and slid down our steep driveway on Flexible Flyers.

At this point in her story, I stopped Carolee and asked, "Have you ever seen the movie *Now and Then*? It's about four women who go back to where they grew up as adults. It tells the story of the summer they all lived on the same cul-de-sac when they were 12 years old. This is your story, too!" Carolee nodded and continued on with her story.

As we grew older, my best friend and I watched longingly at the neighbor boy who delivered our evening newspaper while riding his two wheel bike without hands. We lathered on Panama Jack sunscreen and laid in the sun for hours. Many a night, we snuck out of our back door during sleepover parties to run around with the neighborhood kids. Naturally, my brothers and I fought like cats and dogs over whose turn it was to do which chore when our parents weren't home. But, we always had them done and were busy studying when they pulled in the driveway after work.

We went to church on Sundays and spent most holidays with my grandparents. Every Christmas Eve, my grandfather made whiskey sours in the blender and let us kids sneak a sip. By the time we got to church at midnight, he would promptly fall asleep. When he started snoring, Grandma would nudge him awake and he would immediately start singing a Christmas carol – any carol – regardless of what was happening in the service. Of course, we had to stifle giggles as my dad sternly gave us that warning look to behave or else!

Occasionally out of town family members would come for a visit. And, we always took a summer vacation either to some historical destination (Gettysburg, Philadelphia, old forts, and other boring places to our young minds) or to visit my aunt, uncle, and cousins in southern Florida. They had a key lime tree in their back yard and authentic key lime pie is still my favorite dessert.

It was at this point in her story that Carolee's tone began to change. Little by little, it seemed her rose-colored world was beginning to fade. She continued...

I was very blessed to have everything I needed growing up. Creature comforts that is. Like I said, on the outside, it was all one big happy family. On the inside, not always so.

My older brother was the nerdy science kid. Jim is one of the smartest people I know. My big brother could take apart an old television with all those tiny wires and pieces in the back and put it back together again without ever looking at an instruction manual.

I was the quiet one, always reading a book, riding my bike, going for a walk, or studying. I was the "smart one."

My little brother, Robert, was the sports kid. He loved baseball from the time he was old enough to hold a ball. My dad had played football in high school and could not have been more thrilled.

The problem was that meant Jim was left on the sidelines. Jim and I were never encouraged to get involved with anything, since we were not interested in sports. I am probably the most uncoordinated person you would ever meet when it comes to sports anyway. That being said, Jim got in with the wrong crowd at school, causing many headaches as a teen for my parents. He constantly skipped school, hung out with the drug dealers, and got in trouble. He was so smart though, that he could still skate through school with decent grades!

My sheltered eyes were sure opened one night when Jim asked me to go out with him, his girlfriend Linda, and her best friend Tina. His girlfriend's best friend just happened to be the daughter of our church's secretary. So, of course, my parents thought this was an excellent choice of friends. She had a cute younger brother, Mark, who I had a big crush on at 13 years old!

Little did I know where we were going that night. We wound up in the loft over the secretary's garage where the windowsills were lined with bottles of booze. Packs of cigarettes sat beside overflowing ash trays on the tray tables. I was so shocked. I did not drink or smoke a thing as I watched the older kids do so! Finally, Mark took my hand and we just sat in a corner and talked. Of course, my brother swore me to secrecy, threatening never to take me anywhere again if I told our parents!

That was the beginning of my first taste of romance. My brother turned 16 that summer and I turned 14, so off we went, this group of five to parks, bowling alleys, and McDonalds. We rode bikes and helped at vacation Bible school. We went to the movies and roller skating. One of my favorite things to do that summer was drive to the Columbus International Airport, where we all climbed up to the flat roof and laid down on our backs, watching the planes land just beyond. We would all talk for hours about far off destinations and all the places we would travel when we were grown-up.

Life moved on through my teenage years. Somewhere along the way, Mark drifted out of my life. Jim had found a whole new set of friends by then. I continued to do my best getting good grades and being the "good girl." By age 15, I was in high school. My class was the first to attend a brand new, modern pilot type of school building with wide open spaces, hallways, and high ceilings. The school was built for a total of six grades with classes of 500 students each. However, when it opened to just the 10th grade, this massive building contained only 220 students and related staff. It actually made for a nice situation, because we never experienced the cliques, bullying, or "caste" system so often found during teenage years. I made some new friends with the girls who came from other schools in the area to make up this new one. One good friend had a brother a year older than us. He was so handsome and such a gentleman.

I was instantly in love! I honestly don't remember how he came to notice me, but by the following summer, we were dating.

I remember one of our first dates was to the movie theater to watch *A Star is Born* starring Barbra Streisand and Kris Kristofferson. It was such a sad ending, but had a great soundtrack. My boyfriend gave me the album for Christmas that year and I was even more "in love" with him.

Time marched on and he graduated from high school. I was inducted into the National Honor Society and spent my senior year of high school doing what most girls do to this day. I went to football games, pep rallies, sleepover parties, and dreamed of a future filled with happiness.

Unfortunately, life at home had still not improved. My older brother continued to go down the wrong path filled with drinking and drugs. My younger brother was consumed with sports. My parents did their best to hold our family together despite their mutual dislike of each other. I just stayed in my room, or spent time with my best friend or my boyfriend.

When I graduated from high school, I was very intimidated by the idea of attending college. So many people had filled my ears with talk of parties, drugs, drinking, sexual encounters, and more, that I was scared to even think about being a part of that scene. Nobody actually talked about the education side of it. More than that, I wanted to be an elementary school teacher and unfortunately during that period in history, there simply were no jobs to be had for teachers. I convinced myself that I should just go to work and make a decision about school later.

Keep in mind that when I graduated high school in the 1970's it was not as important for women to attend college immediately, if at all.

Some of the traditional choices, such as getting married or becoming a secretary, were still considered appropriate choices. The women's rights movement had barely begun at that point.

Since my boyfriend was already out of school and had a well paying job, we talked of marriage. We also found ourselves becoming more and more intimate. By late summer, I discovered I was going to have a baby. We were ecstatic and immediately moved up our plans to marry to the following month. Unfortunately, God had other plans in mind.

With tears in her eyes, I had to lean forward to hear Carolee explain this next part of her story.

During a doctor visit, I was told the baby was deformed and dying and I would be risking both our lives if the pregnancy continued. Talk about the most agonizing decision anyone should ever have to make. All our parents persuaded us that the best choice would be to terminate the pregnancy, because as they said, there will be other babies, but only if I survived. As faith-filled parents, I sometimes wonder if this "cleansing procedure" (as everyone called it), was because the baby was already gone and nobody wanted to tell me. I wish someone would have just told me!

To this day, this is my biggest regret in life. There are many times all these years later that I wonder what could have been with this child who never got the chance to live. I did have a doctor tell me several years ago that I should stop worrying about it. That eventually we both would have died anyway had I continued with the pregnancy. But it really doesn't make it any better in the end.

Carolee paused at this point and wiped her eyes before going on.

Well, we did end up marrying in the church I grew up in and had the reception in the church basement complete with cake and fruit punch, so common for the times. We moved into a little one-bedroom apartment near my grandparents and set up housekeeping.

That marriage lasted exactly six months. About a month after our wedding, my husband found an alternate lifestyle. One where he became very angry and could not stop blaming me for "killing his child." One night, I just could not take it any longer and I went into the bathroom and stared in the mirror. I took a bottle of aspirin out of the medicine cupboard and dumped the contents into my palm.

Then Carolee did something unexpected. She smiled!

It was that exact moment that I heard the first of many God-whispers. A voice distinct as anyone standing right beside me whispered in my ear, "Not now. You will be fine."

It wasn't like I thought I had seen a ghost or was hearing voices in my own head. A sense of peace came over me and I knew what to do. I put the aspirin back in the bottle, closed it, returned it to the cabinet and went to bed. The next day, I called my parents and told them I was moving home.

And, I did.

By this point, I was working as a secretary for a large corporation downtown and had made some wonderful friends. I was still in touch with many high school girlfriends. One such friend had an older brother who she insisted on introducing to me. (Yes, I know…) Well one thing led to another and within a year, we were married.

I could really pick the winners! I fell for his sweet talking promises of a life full of family and rich rewards of love. That lasted less than two years, once I found out how many other women he was telling the same thing on the side! So out he went, leaving me with maxed out credit cards and a broken-down car.

It took me an entire year working as a secretary full time during the day and as a night manager at a women's clothing boutique during the evenings to climb my way out of the debt. But during that time, I made a promise to myself that no more would I be fooled by promises of a family, love, and security by a man!

I was 22 years old.

"Wait," I interrupted Carolee before she could continue. "What happened to your brothers?"

Oh, yes. Well ironically Jim decided his path out of trouble was to join the Army! Fortunately, that was the best decision he could have made. He perfected his mechanical engineering skills and found a much better outlet for his intelligence. Robert went on to college and married his high school sweetheart.

"Are they happy?" I asked. Before going on with her story, Carolee smiled and said they were.

The following year, I went to work for an insurance estimating and repair company. I thought there could be nothing more boring! But, I stayed with this company for the next 10 years and met some of the most wonderful people anyone would be lucky to have in their corner. Many are still my friends to this day. One couple met, married, and eventually became my daughter's Godparents. But I'm getting ahead of myself.

Right about this time, my parents finally threw in the towel and divorced. I promised myself at that moment that I would never stay in an unhappy marriage for the sake of keeping my family intact for my children. Maybe if my parents had not thought that was the best thing to do, I would not have wanted to escape and try to find my own happy marriage at such a young age – twice!

Anyway, back to my job. One of the best benefits was they had a tuition reimbursement program. Eventually, I enrolled in college and worked toward a bachelor's degree. I enjoyed every minute of this endeavor and know that I excelled because it was finally time for me to get an education on my terms. It was like a competition with myself to get good grades and have the experience paid for by my employer.

This company was primarily made up of male employees, due to the nature of sales, building inspectors, and repairmen. Again, this was during a time when women were still considered best at being secretaries and general office help. I loved being one of the few women, as I always felt I had better relationships with men as friends than women. Women can be so jealous and catty; men don't want the drama! There was a local neighborhood bar around the corner from the office and we would often times walk over after work and have a few beers. My best friend from junior high worked nearby and we would alternate Friday nights between this bar and one her co-workers frequented. These times made for long conversations and the beginnings of many friendships.

One of those friendships was with one of the inspectors at the office. Tom was married and had a beautiful wife. They longed for a family of their own and they eventually became pregnant. But his wife promptly left him! He was devastated, as he loved the thought of being a family man. I spent a lot of time listening to his woes. One night he admitted it was truly over and he would just have to be a father to his new child from afar.

Some time later, he asked me to dinner. I remember asking, "Like on a real date? With me?!" And he said yes. He took me to one of the oldest, most romantic steak and seafood restaurants in town where I ordered the lobster tail dinner, not understanding what "market price" actually meant. Seeing the top steak dinner on the menu was just $22, and knowing this man was successful, I thought to myself, "How much can a lobster tail dinner be anyway?" So I ordered it!

When the bill arrived, Tom hesitantly showed it to me. $43. I said, "That's not bad considering I had lobster, you had steak, and we each had a glass of wine." He said, "That's just for your dinner!" I was so embarrassed! I offered to pay for my dinner and he of course said that wasn't necessary. I'm telling you this, because he really could not afford it. He was simply a gentleman and did not want to admit it.

He and I continued to date, even though I was very resistant due to his family situation. I was not going to become involved with a married man, one going through a divorce or not! My faith had been growing and I was attending a singles group at my church during this time, as well. I was really exploring my religious beliefs and could not forget about my God-whisper from long ago.

One night around this time, I awoke from a deep sleep in my apartment where I lived alone. As I became more coherent, I realized that as I was sleeping on my right side, there was someone laying on my other side with their arm around me. The most peaceful feeling came over me as I became more aware of the sensation. Then I began to panic! Who is in bed with me? What should I do? All of a sudden, I flipped over to see. Nobody was there.

As I settled down, I realized I had just experienced another God-whisper and I should concentrate on remembering the feeling of complete peacefulness.

As time went on, I continued to work, go to school, make friends, and spend time with family, friends, and church gatherings. I rode my bike often and read lots of books. I went to parties and worked on craft projects. Tom eventually divorced and we became even closer. However, he had been so hurt from the loss of his last love that he continually told me he never wanted to marry or have more children. I expressed that I did want those things, but for the time being, I would continue seeing him.

That very same New Year's Eve, he took me out for a romantic dinner and proposed.

I remember distinctly responding, "But you don't want to get married again." To which he replied, "But I don't want you to marry anyone else." I just looked at him in wonder and he asked, "So is that a yes?" It was a yes. I was 28 years old.

As often times happen when you are with someone with children and ex-spouses, there were many ups and downs over the next several years. My friends thought I was crazy to want to marry someone in that situation. I always felt that at my age, I could have children, too. I would expect someone who wanted to marry me to accept them, as well. So why wouldn't I feel the same about a man? Eventually we did marry and started a life together. It had been 10 years since the end of my last marriage.

Within six months, my husband was offered a high-level position in another city about two hours away from our families. We talked it over and agreed it was worth the move. His little daughter was in elementary school, played soccer, and belonged to a dance team. We had formed a good relationship with her mother who agreed to work out the logistics with all the family dynamics of a blended family. This woman never questioned my loyalty to her daughter as I had long ago assured her if I had a child with a step-mother in the picture that I would hope that person would love my child in my absence. For nearly 30 years since, that's what I have always tried my best to do, which has made for a good relationship for all of us.

Life was good in our new city. We bought a home, made new friends, and traveled often. We continued to spend as much time as possible with our little girl, Kate, as well as family and old friends. We had an old boat we would take to the lake on the weekends and enjoyed many good times with friends, old and new, visiting islands and listening to bands on the weekends.

After a few years of marriage, my husband said he was ready to start a family with me. I was very hesitant as I wanted to be sure it would be something different for him and that he would be a very "hands-on" parent. We had no family in the area and I did not want to be alone as a "stay-at-home" mom. Tom assured me he had always wanted to be that type of father, but had never been afforded the chance. He was really looking forward to it.

Well, it took awhile, but I eventually became pregnant. Right about that time my husband started travelling five days a week for a new promotion he had received at work. However, we were both overjoyed at the thought of becoming parents together. Nine months later, our beautiful baby girl, Beth entered the world.

And he became a different person.

At first, he really tried to be a good father by holding her and feeding her. But he could not endure crying or diapers, late night feedings or any of the unpleasant parts that come with babies. It was my job to keep her quiet. And to keep the peace for him.

Two days after our daughter Beth's sixth birthday, my brother-in-law abruptly passed away. He and my husband had experienced a rocky relationship through the years and this loss put my husband into a position of the unknown. It really took a toll on him. As well as our marriage.

Rather than address the erosion of our lives, we both started living separate lives in the same household. I became involved with Beth's upbringing and started my own business. He continued to travel through the week and busied himself with hobbies on the weekends.

Once again I stopped Carolee. "You haven't told me anymore of your God whispers," I said. "Oh, I did forget about one actually," she remembered.

She went on to tell me about a terrible dream she had been having when Beth was two years old.

I would dream Beth would be near the edge of an ocean, or a pool, or a lake. She would turn around and look at me with a big grin. Then, she would run ahead and into the water as I called after her to stop. But I could never reach Beth before she went out of sight. One morning, I was drinking coffee at the kitchen table wondering what this could possibly mean and why was I experiencing this dream so often. I heard Beth's little toddler legs running up behind me. As she tugged on my arm, she said, "Mommy. Don't worry. I am fine."

How did this baby girl know? I never had the dream again. And I'm positive that was all God!

So, the years marched on. We experienced the loss of more family members and a few friends, but also the joy of weddings and milestone birthdays. We did our best to celebrate holidays and Kate's high school graduation before she moved west to attend college. We took a few trips together as a family, but more often, took separate vacations.

By the time my mother passed away nine years later, we were living completely separate lives. Kate was married and lived on the other side of the country. I was speaking to professional, church, and networking groups about finding peace as busy women living in the "sandwich generation." The one where you are caring for your children, parents, and yourselves. Little did anyone know how the peace I spoke of was completely absent from my own life.

Much to my surprise, I received recognition from local magazines and won some awards for my "expertise." My five minutes of fame was short-lived, as is often the case. But my baby was going to turn 16 years old and I wanted to do something really special to celebrate. Beth also wanted to do something special. You see, throughout her lifetime, this child of mine had always looked for ways to help others in need.

During Hurricane Katrina relief efforts, she designed a button and sold it for donations. She was barely six years old. Often times, she asked for donations to the Toys for Tots program instead of receiving birthday gifts. Following the Boston Marathon bombing, she created a fashion show to raise money for victims. On the occasion of her 16th birthday, she was inspired to raise funds to buy Christmas gifts for every one of the 500 under-represented community school children at a local elementary school.

On the other hand, I planned a surprise family birthday party for Beth at a restaurant in our hometown, as well as one at our home with her friends. Since her birthday is mid-November, we also hosted Thanksgiving that year with about ten people. As usual, I was planning our annual Christmas party, where about forty friends attended at our home every year in mid-December.

And my marriage was continuing to crumble by the day.

Between working, party planning, the holidays, and keeping the house in order, needless to say, I was exhausted! I was so extremely tired and had a sinus infection that would not go away. I kept pushing through, thinking I would take care of myself in the new year, when I would have time to rest and re-group.

But then it all fell apart.

"When Esther's words were reported to Mordecai, he sent back this answer: "Do not think that because you are in the king's house you alone of all the Jews will escape. For if you remain silent at this time, relief and deliverance for the Jews will arise from another place, but you and your father's family will perish.

And who knows but that you have come to your royal position for such a time as this?

Then Esther sent this reply to Mordecai: "Go, gather together all the Jews who are in Susa, and fast for me. Do not eat or drink for three days, night or day. I and my attendants will fast as you do. When this is done, I will go to the king, even though it is against the law. And if I perish, I perish."

Esther 4:12-16, The Bible (NIV)

Chapter Two
Three Little Words

12/12 Day One

"You have leukemia."

What? No! I am anemic or have a severe sinus infection. Wait. What exactly is leukemia? It's cancer, right? No, it's some weird blood disorder. It's deadly though, isn't it? This is not happening. That's not what she said. Is it? Oh no, Beth!

Within ten seconds of those three little words, these are the thoughts that flashed through my mind.

Without missing a beat, this doctor standing beside me in a ten by twelve examination room started asking me questions and rattling off instructions: Do you know any oncologists? You need to get to a hospital right away. Let me get my list. Stay there.

In a flash, she was back with a clipboard, thumbing through pages.

What is happening??? This just is not possible. Why would she be telling me this in this way if it were really true? I think I need to sit down. My head is literally spinning.

She went on. OK, here's a list of oncologists. What hospital do you want to go to? You need to get there now!

In what felt like slow motion, I finally spoke. "Um, Northeast Medical Hospital? I had elbow surgery there once and they were nice. Let me see your list." In a blur, I looked at the list of doctor names and stopped at the name Estherlyn. "Well, Esther is my favorite book in the Bible, so close enough - let's go with her."

The doctor spun around again and said she would call and see what she could do. By the grace of God, she was back in what seemed like 30 seconds and reported this doctor would take me, but I needed to get to the hospital immediately. "Oh, and you might want to take an overnight bag" was the last thing she said to me.

At this point, I found my voice and said to Carolee, "Why in the world would she have told you all of that without anyone there with you? I can't even imagine how you felt!" Carolee just shrugged her shoulders and continued.

Well, it was strange. But anyway, just as quick, I walked out of that office, got in my car, and drove the ten minutes back to my home.

I walked in the door and Tom just looked and me and asked, "What?"

"She said I have leukemia."

He stood there with a look on his face as stunned as I felt. Since one of us needed to act, I asked, "Where's Beth?" "Upstairs doing homework."

"OK, well, I'm going to take a shower and pack an overnight bag. Under no uncertain terms are you to say the word *leukemia* to her."

You see, Beth had a classmate pass away from leukemia just that spring. It had left a profound sadness in her at the thought of losing someone to such a deadly disease.

I went into my bedroom and closed the door. After standing motionless for a minute or so, I picked up my phone and called my church minister. His first comment after hearing my diagnosis was, "Well, here's a new chapter for your life!" Of course, he prayed for me and offered assistance from himself or anyone I needed.

Next, I called a cherished friend who was also a minister. She was completely heartbroken at the news and cried out in prayer immediately. We talked for a few minutes and then I decided to take a shower, since I had spent the day decorating and cleaning for our Christmas party the next night.

The last call I made was to a friend who had been battling cancer for nearly ten years. "Ann, what should I do?" I will never forget her advice. "Whatever you do, do not let them rush you!"

When I had packed a few things in my overnight travel bag, we told Beth that I needed to go to the hospital for some tests to find out what was going on. She insisted on going with us, as she had barely ever been away from me her whole life.

Off we went. When we arrived, we were ushered to the third floor. They certainly were waiting for me. Instantly, a nurse came in and started asking questions. Name, birthdate, height, weight, was I pregnant, any underlying health problems, medications, etc., etc., etc. Then before I knew it she blurted out, "Well when you have *leukemia,* you know you will be here a long time, don't you?" Oh my goodness. Beth instantly burst into tears and I am sure if looks could kill, that nurse would have been dead on the spot! I called out to Beth, "Come here, honey. It's going to be fine. C'mon, let's stay positive." She was inconsolable. Finally, her dad took her by the hand and they left the room. They came back a few minutes later and she was glued to my side the remainder of the night.

I'm guessing you have never had a bone marrow biopsy? I am hoping that your answer is no and that would always be your answer. Let me say it is likely the most painful thing I have ever endured, mentally or physically! I squeezed my eyes shut and gripped the hand of a young nurse so tightly, she finally asked me if I could let go a little. That made me feel worse!

As always with tests, the next hours were just waiting and watching the clock tick by the minutes. Then the hours. Until Beth and I finally drifted off to sleep.

I really felt like this part of Carolee's story was too much for her to explain, so I told her so. The next time Carolee and I met, she handed me a file folder of papers. When I asked why, she told me she had been keeping a dairy of sorts throughout the rest of her cancer experience. And since I was right in saying it was too much for her to share, she wanted me to read and tell this part on my own. Here is what Carolee wrote.

12/13 Day Two

Hi everyone! Due to a family emergency, unfortunately our Christmas party tonight is cancelled... Carolee has been admitted to the hospital, has been diagnosed with leukemia and she is beginning treatments as of today. We wanted to send this message out to you, her closest friends, to ask for your prayers for her healing and recovery. Carolee wants us to send you her love.

It's Friday. We are supposed to be hosting about 40 people at our house for a Christmas party tonight. Well, that's not going to happen. My husband and daughter composed a text, took my phone and sent out a message to folks to let them know what was happening and the party was cancelled. Much to my horror, I discovered they had sent it to many people who had not been invited to the party. But it really didn't matter. What people wanted to know was how could they help. Pray. Pray is the only thing to do.

Beth and I woke up that morning on the tiniest single size bed you can imagine, with tear stains on our pillows. But as I looked down at this darling girl and kissed the top of her head, I could feel the warmth of prayers for all who knew where I was, what I was going through, and what was potentially coming. And that was the end of the peace for day two! It was 7 AM and the flurry of activity was just beginning. First came the "transportation" person who said we had to get some tests and I said, "What about Beth?" He was followed by a kind nurse named Angel (ironically) who came in and said, "We've got her. No need to worry." (Tom had gone back home to get some rest overnight.)

So as the saying goes, I was poked and prodded and x-rayed and more, for about the next four hours. By that point I asked someone to find my husband. When they did, I asked him to call Ann and see if she thought things were going too fast? He called her and tried to explain to the best that he could what was happening with me. She assured him this was exactly what needed to happen. And that I would be fine. So another four or five tests later and several hours went by when this nice technician came back once again to wheel me back to my room on the third floor of this massive hospital that I would soon learn was going to be my home for quite some time.

Exhausted after an entire day of tests, at about 5 PM Friday night my oncologist came in and said it was just as we expected: *acute myeloid leukemia*. "We're starting you on two types of chemotherapy." Dr. Estherlyn explained, "One known as the 'red devil' for three days and the other is just standard chemotherapy which you will have for seven days." I asked then would I be going home? And she just shook her head and continued, "No. You'll be hooked up to these 24 hours a day, monitored closely for infections, and then there will be seven days with no treatment, another bone marrow biopsy, and then we will see where things are at that point." *Then what?* And she said, "Well the idea is to force your body into remission." *And what if it doesn't?* She looked away and ever so slightly shook her head from left to right, looked at me again and said, "Then there would be nothing else we can do."

And I said, "OK."

12/14 Day Three

Somehow I had dozed back off to sleep after being hooked up to port and IV lines and got used to the fact that this pole and these tubes would be connected to me for the next seven days or 168 hours! Recognition of my surroundings became clear when I looked on my bedside table to find a note from a wise woman who I had a admired from afar for many years through a business connection. This woman was a highly respected attorney in our community and one of the most faithful people I had ever met - nor have ever met to this day. She stopped by and finding me asleep, had taken a business card and written on the back:

Praying for you with love and trusting in Him.

I cherished that card and held it close throughout the entire day. Clinging to these words with hope.

12/15 Day Four

I'll never forget when I woke up Sunday morning, my two best friends in the world, along with their husbands, were standing at the foot of my bed. *What are you doing here?* "Oh, I could not sleep," Rose said. "So about 4AM, I looked at Steve and said, 'Get up. We have to get to Carolee! Now!' So, here we are."

Then Jean said, "Oh my gosh. This is terrible. It's just like the movie *Beaches*!" Rubbing the sleep out of my eyes, I burst out laughing, then wiped away tears. "It's going to be fine," I assured their worried faces.

And I meant it. Somehow, in just 48 hours, the prayers being spoken for me were coming through loud and clear.

I could feel them. Have you ever had that happen? A sense of utter peace starts at the crown of your head and travels all the way down to the tips of your toes. It is at once the strangest and also the best feeling you can imagine. Pure peace in knowing you are loved and no matter what happens, it will be fine.

Before they left later that morning, Rose pressed a small wooden cross into my palm. "I want you to keep this. My mom gave it to me a long time ago when I was having a hard time. I would cling to it so often and it brought me such comfort. But, I want it back one day. One day when you feel better, are fully recovered, and have felt the pure love gained from the hope it will bring you. You can give it back to me then."

12/16 Day Five

It's Monday and the weekend calm became a storm of activity in my new corner of the world. An infectious disease doctor stopped by my room to let me know he would be working hand in hand with my oncologist. Just that morning, I had asked Dr. Estherlyn if it was true that usually the cancer doesn't kill you. Instead it's the inability to recover from the infections you catch with a compromised immune system. She agreed that was often the case. So, I was very relieved to meet this new doctor. Once again, a round of questions, poking and prodding ensued. I guess once you have given birth, not to mention wondering if your life was soon to end, you no longer care about modesty! There was no longer any such thing.

I had begun to experience horrible mouth sores which proved difficult to talk, eat, or swallow. The nurses were wonderful to explain anything and everything I was experiencing to me. The 'red devil' chemo was known to cause this side effect. It was miserable. Later I would learn most patients would have such bad mouth sores, they would travel all the way down their throats and make it difficult to breathe. I soon realized how much worse my situation could be. And how once again, prayers were being answered. If all I could do was not talk on the phone or choke down a sandwich, I really had nothing to complain about!

Fortunately, I was able to have technology with me so I had my phone and my iPad. That iPad saved my sanity! It was my lifeline with the outside world. I don't know how people handled the isolation in a situation like this prior to these types of technology devices at their fingertips. It probably was only five or six years since you had to rely on a hardwired bedside table telephone to communicate with the outside world. Even then, those phone calls were charged to your account every time you used one. Often they were not even available in every room. Anyway I got my iPad out and started the first of many emails to a small group of people that slowly grew from about my close circle of 10 or so people to over 100 during the next several months. And then I'm not even sure how many of those people shared the information with others, but I know they did. The peace that came from prayers being lifted for me is indescribable to this day.

I sent the very first one on this day:

Hi to all my wonderful family & friends. Below is the latest update. Would you mind forwarding to other friends and family, and anyone else you think might want to know and would be willing to pray? (I don't have a lot of email addresses on my iPad.) That is our biggest need at the moment.

We are trusting in the care I am receiving here at Northeast Medical Hospital. I really like my oncologist, Dr. Estherlyn (thought it was good that Esther is one of my heroes from the Bible). She is always smiling and very willing to spend any amount of time answering questions. She is one of the "best of the best" I understand in the field of oncology in our city.

For all you medical people, my numbers are this today: red blood 7.7, white blood 1.1 (this number has to get to zero to get rid of the leukemia cells), platelets 15. I have AML or Acute Myeloid Leukemia.

They have been giving me so many infection preventative drugs, I couldn't begin to tell you what all of it is. They are working though. And, there is this miracle drug that the second I feel nauseous, they give it to me and I am fine. No hair loss yet, but that is coming. Maybe I'll get some waves when it comes back... A lifelong wish of mine.

I apologize for not answering every text, voice mail, and email. It is amazing how fast the time goes here with a constant parade of doctors, nurses, dietitians, housekeeping, tests, etc. My favorite are the "transportation" people who wheel me around. So funny they are called that. I would be awful at that job since I can't even steer a hotel luggage cart without banging up the walls.

Please keep the well wishes, prayers, texts, emails, cards, whatever, coming. It is such an amazing comfort and I know it's what is keeping me feeling good, as well as comforting Tom, Beth, Kate, and family.

Love,

Carolee

12/17 Day Six: You are filled with grace

Today I woke up to this text on my phone from my thoughtful Mama. For the rest of the time I spent in my new "home," she sent me an encouraging word or two every single morning. It's what a mother does who loves her children most of all, even when she's a stepmother. How lucky am I for mine.

12/18 Day Seven: A loving heart

One more day. Just one more day of this pole being attached to my arm! It's funny how fast you get used to something, but how much you long for it to end when that end is in sight.

12/19 Day Eight: Faith-filled

Woohoo! Free from that IV pole and chemo infusions! I asked, *Can I go home now?*

"Well, no. Remember, now you wait. We have to wait seven days to find out if your body has been forced into remission. We have to check your blood counts daily. We have to make sure it's as gone as possible and wait until your immune system recovers."

Oh. That's right.

It's six days till Christmas. I have nothing wrapped. I have a stack of Christmas cards ready to send.

Beth is home on Christmas break from school.

And my husband is spiraling out of control.

I squeezed my eyes shut tight and silently cried out to God, *HELP!*

12/20 Day Nine: Strong

Well, how ironic is this word? I am definitely trying to be. My poor baby called me today and is trying so hard herself to be strong. It's very difficult when she can't drive, her father won't bring her to see me, and everyone is busy getting ready for Christmas. My heart nearly broke in two when she called, choking back tears with a muffled, "Mommy, please come home. I can't take it anymore." She has been doing her best to take over my role and keep Tom calm. This is just not something a child should have to do. And it's six more days until we find out my fate. Prayers have never been more needed nor necessary than now. Not for me, but for Beth. For my survival to bring balance back to her life.

12/21 Day Ten: Enveloped in love

After yesterday, I decided it was time to reach back out to my faithful team of prayer warriors.

Good morning,

It's been a few days and I thought I would update you on progress and set backs so far.

But, first I have to say that I could not stop crying this morning as the overwhelming outpouring of love from people far and wide finally hit me. I have received so many cards, emails, Facebook messages, and gifts (some from people I don't know but suspect are church and community members) that my heart was just overflowing with gratitude. I know I have not acknowledged them all, but they are appreciated more than I can say.

Anyway, the seven day chemo is done and I am free from my IV cart that has been my constant companion since Dec. 13th. The numbers are good for now. White is down to 0.4 (this is the number they watch for leukemia - best will be 0.1 or 0.2), red at 9.7 (needs to stay over 8) and platelets at 8 (I'll get a dose of those today because they don't like it under ten). It's such an interesting process. They draw blood every morning to get the number counts. But, the true numbers won't be known until the next bone marrow biopsy which will be Dec. 26th. That shows the truth regarding the presence or not of any leukemia cells. I asked why the delay since they stopped chemo last night and were told that it's like an antibiotic that you take. Even though you take it all, it is still working in your system for several days to follow. Same for chemo. So, time will tell.

In the meantime, I had a fever yesterday which brings on a whole flurry of activity and tests. They even come in with a huge machine that takes a chest x-ray right from your bed! Everything turned out fine and my temperature was back to normal two hours later. It's comforting when they go overboard at the slightest risk! I have to say that every person on this floor has been wonderful. Very attentive and just nice people.

However, here is a new prayer request. I have developed a bacterial infection of the digestive system called c-diff. If you look it up, it sounds devastating. I actually feel fine, just have to literally run to the restroom often (which needs to stop and stop quickly). This brought on all new antibiotics including one I drink that tastes like something I'm sure I've had as a bar "shot" back in the day. Kind of a tart honey lemon flavor. So this is my new prayer request. Not only that the leukemia will be gone when they do the biopsy next week, but also that this infection will be wiped out quickly (not so easy without an immune system) with no more infections. I once again said to the infectious doctor that I have heard more often than not that it's not the cancer that kills you, but the infections you catch. He agreed.

Beth and Tom are hanging in there. Those of you who know Tom well know that he just does not do well in times of crisis, change, or breaks in his routine. If you know Beth well, you know she thrives on calm, loving and caring situations. They are doing their best without me there as the third piece of the mix to keep us all balanced. I know they are reaching the end of their ability to keep their chins up, especially this time of year. They are scared, out of sorts, and missing me at home. Even our cats are acting weird, they tell me. It is nice to know that I am missed and so loved. Please pray that they will find comfort with each other and feel the peace of God's loving arms around them. We have wonderful friends who are doing everything to care for them and keep them distracted from the reality of all of this, which is such a comfort to me.

Kate keeps us smiling with a constant stream of new pictures and videos of James from Seattle. Our sweet grandson is 10 months old and as adorable as ever. They plan to visit in January and I can not wait to see my other girl and her family. What a relief it is to be connected to the outside world through technology. I keep thinking how it wasn't long ago that I would have been stuck here with just a hard wired phone as my only lifeline to everyone.

We're keeping visitors to the bare minimum because infection is such a great possibility. Nobody is allowed in who hasn't had a flu shot anyway. My parents came from Columbus yesterday, bringing another room full of love and comfort. Otherwise, just Tom and Beth, our ministers, and a couple of close friends who have been bringing Beth here when Tom is working, are my only visitors. I have a ton of mouth sores which makes it difficult to talk anyway (so annoying, but they have "magic mouthwash" - not kidding, that's what it's called - to help).

So, here is my constant vision. Remember the Bible story where the woman is trying to get through the crowd to reach Jesus? I keep seeing her reaching for the hem of His robe and He finally turns and smiles at her. I am keeping focused on reaching His hem and seeing Him turn to smile at me.

Thank you is so little to say for all you are doing for us. Wishing you a wonderful weekend as you finish getting ready for Christmas.

Love,

Carolee

12/22 Day Eleven: Cherished

I had a heart to heart talk with my husband today on the phone. I told him that I did not want him, nor Beth to be with me when Dr. Estherlyn gave me the news of my leukemia status on December 26th. Instead, I asked my parents to come and be with me. He said fine, but they could not stay at our house, even though a blizzard is predicted and they live a three hour car drive away in good weather! But, I told him that would be okay with me. I needed to hear the news with people I know would be there for me and Beth, no matter the outcome. And, if it was bad news, there was no way I was letting him give that to Beth.

12/23 Day Twelve: In God's shining light

I just focused on Mama's words today. There wasn't much else to do. Sigh.

12/24 Day Thirteen: A gift to me

Tom and Beth arrived around noon and brought me an helium filled Christmas tree balloon! I just laughed out loud when Beth said, "We brought you a Christmas tree, Mom! You needed one!" Yes, I did actually. That tree stayed in my room until I went home much later, bringing a smile every time I glanced at it or someone visiting commented about it.

Fortunately my good friend Debbie had offered to help wrap a couple of gifts I had at home for Tom and Beth. I had instructed her to ask them to bring them to the hospital today. Beth had only asked for new designer boots that year, so I made sure that was what she opened that morning with us. Honestly, I don't know what I had her wrap for Tom. A sweater, I think!

Before I was diagnosed, I had mentioned that I wanted an exercise bracelet that would track my steps. Knowing I was going to need to keep my oxygen levels up by walking, that's exactly what Tom and Beth gave me that day.

I insisted they not spend Christmas Eve with me, but with good friends who had offered to host them for dinner that night. I had to make sure that Beth had some kind of decent Christmas and I knew this family would do that for her.

All in all, it was a good day.

12/25 Day Fourteen: Watched over by angels

Oh my goodness! All day I received texts and emails from family and friends near and far! I was astonished at business acquaintances who told me they asked their entire family to remember me in prayer. What a lesson for me to realize how much other people genuinely pray when you simply ask. Even for people they don't know, nor probably ever would. Did I ever need to start that practice myself!

One of my favorite texts came with a gorgeous sun-filled Wyoming mountain scene. My dear friend was at her family home in the mountains for Christmas. The text explained that for several days, she had been very sad thinking about me laying in a hospital bed, not knowing my fate. It had been cloudy and dismal there in Wyoming. But on Christmas morning, she awoke early and took her coffee outside to look at the mountain. There, the sun rose and shined out God's radiant love. The text said, "This is your mountain! Merry Christmas and much good news in the week to come." What an incredible gift of the reminder that God shows his love in many ways. We just need to look.

12/26 Day Fifteen: Blast-free!!

My parents arrived at eight o'clock this morning. They must have been up since four! But, they walked into my room smiling ear-to-ear, bringing a soft blanket, chocolates, and love that could literally be felt the minute they passed through the doorway. We sat around and waited for hours for Dr. Estherlyn to call. When she finally did, we could hear her smiles. "It's good! It's good!" she cried. "You're going to be fine!"

I don't even know what she said after that. All I could think about was thanking God. Thinking about Beth. A whirl of thoughts of what would come next. What I needed to do. Then, a calm relief. Whew!

Amazingly, Tom did not bother to call until late that night to ask what had happened. And as soon as he heard the news, that was the last I saw of him until New Year's Day.

<u>12/27 Day Sixteen: Awesome!</u>

Thought I better update my cheerleaders with the news!

Good afternoon,

I hope this finds each of you with warm memories of a nice Christmas this week with your loved ones. It was definitely a different one for me and my family than ever before. It actually made me take time to stop and relax, reflecting on so many of you, just how blessed my life is, and once again thanking God for all of it.

We have been in waiting mode for the past week when the chemo stopped. Dr. Estherlyn came in yesterday to perform the second bone marrow biopsy. Not nearly as bad as the first one (or maybe I am just a little more used to all the poking, tests, etc. that goes on continuously here).

Yesterday, they called us around 3PM and said the 'flit' test was good, along with the blasts numbers. No idea what a flit test is and this morning the doctor said it's not that important to know, just that good is good.

This morning, Dr. Estherlyn came in with all smiles and said the most important part of the biopsy came back showing *no leukemia*. PRAISE GOD! There are two more test results they are waiting on. One should be back over the weekend and the other one could take up to two more weeks (it's a chromosome study to make sure there are no abnormalities or cancer anywhere else in my body). She was confident that they will be good, too.

Let me stop here and say that without all of the prayers from all of you and everyone you passed the request on to, I honestly don't know if the answer would have been so positive. There is nothing in this life that is more powerful than prayer and a positive attitude. I am more sure of that now than ever before. Thank you is such a small thing to say given the huge amount of appreciation I have for you.

Dr. Estherlyn said, "I couldn't be more pleased. You are one of the good ones." I know she was referring to the fact that I followed her orders to a 't' but I also know that phrase will be with me for a long time to come. It makes my heart smile.

So, going forward, they watch my blood counts to make sure everything is headed back in the right direction. Then, in ten days to two weeks, I can go home. Then, two weeks later, back here for five days of what they call "consolidation" chemo, then back home. If all goes well, I go through that routine two more times to stay in remission. After that, they do regular blood tests.

This truly is the best case scenario. I am still in danger of infection, fevers, relapse, etc., until all these treatments are done. They said I can go about my regular schedule at home, but each of the chemo treatments knocks my immune system out again. So I still can't be around anyone who hasn't had a flu shot when my immune system is down after the chemo treatments. We looked at the calendar and if this all goes according to schedule, I'll be done by the first week in March. I've been told that if you can stay in remission for two years, chances are it won't come back and they have never seen leukemia come back after five years. Continued prayers are so welcome.

Lots of discussions have been going on about why does God let this happen? Why now? Truly I am not a "what if? why me?" type of person. There is a lesson in everything that happens to us. So far, I have realized that when someone is in need, it is more important to drop what you can and go to their side. I can't tell you how many people have done this for us the past two weeks with no regard to the busy time of year, Christmas preparations, or anything else. I have learned that people are more important than to do lists! (Never fear, I'm not giving them up, just decided not to be so tied to them.) I have once again been reminded how very blessed I am to have the family that I do. I am loved beyond compare. And as always, I am glad to be an American living in the USA. I keep thinking of other countries that don't have the medical care, insurance plans, and freedoms to choose their care like we do here.

Last, I received so many wonderful notes about my comment that I was reaching for Jesus' hem, that I wanted to share my new vision. There was an old video on YouTube with scenes of Jesus' teachings, playing to the tune *Mary Did You Know.* (It's no longer available.) But my favorite part was the end of the video as the song came to a close to the lyric "the sleeping child you're holding is the great I Am," and the scene is Jesus walking away, turning with a smile, and motioning you to follow Him.

Wishing you a wonderful New Year with lots of love, happiness and good health.

Love,

Carolee

12/28 Day Seventeen: Amazing

So now what? Not much. That's what! I did start reading a funny book called *Love Does* by Bob Goff. It's very inspiring and I'm underlining things I don't want to forget.

12/29 Day Eighteen: In my heart

A good friend brought Beth to stay with me today. Probably out of boredom, we started listing all the books and movies we had begun noticing where someone in the story was diagnosed with cancer. And not just any cancer, but leukemia! We guessed that's likely because the statistics are not very high for leukemia and maybe the writers felt like they were making people feel better by not making them worry this is something that would ever happen to them. Honestly, if you Google movies and television shows where the character has leukemia, 263 titles appear! (IMBD.com).

What's funny is the movie *Love Story*. I remember watching that not long after it was released on TV years ago. At the time, I never knew "Jenny" had leukemia. But re-watching it, there is nothing else she could have had. The way it was handled medically in the movie was so wrong though! We just laughed out loud at the thought that you would be supplied "white blood cells" intravenously, all the while talking to and kissing your husband one minute and drop over dead the next!

12/30 Day Nineteen: Overflowing with peace, love, and platelets

Watching the clock is like waiting for water to boil! I decided a better use of my time was to write another update.

Good morning,

Well another step forward in my progress with a normal chromosome report. The doctor is 'very positive.'

On another note, my platelets are dwindling which is bringing on a whole new set of issues. My thoughtful friend, Rick, offered the following info to help:

Hello all,

Our hearts go out to Carolee and her family. I know that everyone asks "What can I do?" to help and I have a suggestion. Carolee is having chemotherapy and that is going to require a lot of platelet infusions to counteract the destruction of the normal cells in her blood. Contact the Red Cross and offer to donate platelets. This is done using a procedure called apheresis and it will take about 2 1/2 hours of your time during which you get to stretch out on a comfy sofa and watch television. Platelets have a very short life span so they can't be stockpiled, and she may require 120 such donations.

I'm making my appointment and I encourage you to help Carolee out in this way. It is not possible to specifically donate to Carolee, but your donation will ensure that everyone who needs platelets will receive them.

During this season of family, love, and the generosity of giving, I can't think of a better present for our special friend. Thank You!

Anything you feel called to do will help so many in need. They are having trouble locating platelets for me because the doctor said, 'It's the holidays and nobody donates this time of year.' How ironic that my blood type is B Positive, which is my motto in life!

Ok, I'll write more later. Continued prayers are much needed and truly appreciated.

Love,

Carolee

<u>12/31 Day Twenty: Wrapped in God's love (and of all your family and friends)</u>

It's New Years Eve and very quiet on this third floor wing of the hospital. Somehow, I was awake and it was nearly midnight. One of the nurses came into my room and told me they were all going to watch the downtown fireworks from another window. "Do you want to watch them with us," she asked me. "No, not really," I answered. Somehow, it just didn't seem like there was much to celebrate at that moment.

<u>1/1 Day Twenty-One: Patience, perseverance and optimism</u>

Another new year. I wondered what this one would bring for me and my daughter. Just then, a friend appeared in my hospital room doorway, with Beth right behind her. "Happy New Year, Mom!" she called out. I just love that girl! No matter what mood I'm in, she can always make me smile.

1/5 Day Twenty-Five: A blessing to all who know and love you

Finally! Beth went back to school today. Something to occupy her time and get some normalcy back in her life. We are fortunate to live in a rural area with a small school district. All the kids have gone to school together since kindergarten. And the teaching and administrative staff could not have been kinder. From the beginning of this cancer diagnosis, many had called, texted, or written notes to let me know they were praying for us and asking how they could help. Their care for Beth was more than I could have hoped for.

After reading one such note on my iPad, I looked up at the young nurse taking my vitals and said, "I swear I live in Mayberry RFD!" Of course, she had no idea what I was talking about. All I could think of was *Wow, I am old!* Instead I looked at her and clarified, "Small Town America that is."

1/7 Day Twenty-Seven: Patience and perseverance

About 3:00 this afternoon, one of the nurses came in to check on me. I was reading and glanced up to see a confused look on her face. "Where is your husband these days," she asked. I made up an excuse that he was busy working and taking care of Beth. The truth was that I had no idea. Nor did I really care at that point.

1/10 Day Thirty: Gracious

I'm still just waiting. Not much else to do, so I wrote another update.

Good morning and Happy Friday,

I hope this finds all of you well and off to a great start in the new year.

It's day 30 for me here at Northeast Medical Hospital and although I'm glad to have missed the Arctic blast earlier this week, I sure am ready to go home. I apologize for being out of touch for a while, but I have been waiting until I received the good news that I would be going home. How thrilled I am to let you know that will be tomorrow!

So many of you have asked if the time has seemed endless, if I'm bored, tired, and basically, how I feel in Northeast Medical Hospital. It seems silly to say, but the time has actually passed very quickly for me. My day starts at 6AM and before I feel like I've had time to blink, it's 11AM and then 4PM when I glance at the clock again, and last glance it's 9PM and I am fighting to keep my eyes open! And all this time, I thought at home that my days would fly by like that because I was always so busy. Guess it's true that the older you get, the faster the time goes by.

Overall, I feel great. I do tire easily, so I have learned how to take daytime naps. Not such a bad thing. I am able to work and have been staying in touch with the most amazing clients anyone in business could hope for. Every single one tells me to just get well and they will carry the reins until I want to come back. (Although a couple have said that they know I will recover faster if I still get to boss them around - ha!) Being connected to the outside world through texts, emails, and phone calls has truly saved me. And then a smiling face of a loved one will arrive for a visit or one of the staff here comes in with a big pile of well wishes cards. I have an entire bag full, which I haven't sent home. I love looking through them from time to time and seeing each face of the sender in my mind.

I also am blessed to be surrounded here by the most uplifting hospital staff possible. The head nurse came in a few days ago and said I had been here long enough that she wanted to take a survey of my likes, dislikes, and suggestions for improvement. I thought long and hard before I answered that I honestly couldn't ask for better. I had yet to meet anyone who wasn't kind, respectful, caring, and polite. Everyone from the gal who takes my meal orders by phone (they actually have a restaurant type menu to choose), Sallie the "housekeeper" who is this pleasant single mom with two daughters; Max, our favorite "tech" with teenage sons and a wife who teaches; Amy and Karen, my favorite day nurses (both are married moms with little boys); and Kim, my favorite night nurse (a single mom my age with two teen boys), right up to Dr. Estherlyn herself (a lot of you have written to tell me about personal experiences with her - all positive). I just love her personality, bedside manner, and care.

Exercise is an important part of this healing process and I walk a mile and a half each day through the halls of my little corner of the hospital. I have to wear a surgical mask, which is an entertaining sight with my dwindling amount of hair, but it's interesting to go out and see all the activity that goes on around here beyond my room. If I thought it was a parade of people through my room, it is nothing compared to outside it. I have watched people being picked up to go home by loved ones, people being wheeled in and out for tests, people watching sports from their beds, way too many people who don't close the back of their hospital gowns (even though you can wear your own clothes here, which I have done from the start) to sadly, watching families keep vigil over someone they will soon say goodbye to for the last time. This is my prayer time, where I thank God over and over for the people here, every single one of you, every prayer that has been said on my behalf, and all the positive health news I have received. I pray for others who are experiencing loss, grief, worry, troubles, health issues, cancer battles, and more. I pray for continued good health, complete remission, and no relapse or infection. I often wonder how our amazing God hears it all and answers us all. That is the best part of faith, just believing and letting go of the why's and how's!

Speaking of which, I have a small mountain of reading material here. But, the only thing I have actually read (and I'm still not finished) in the entire month I've been here is a fantastic book that my caring friend Betsy sent to me, *Love Does* by Bob Goff. He is a 50-something attorney in California who tells his life story in short snippets that make the reader laugh out loud. What a life he has led, but the whole message is how he learned that showing love is more important that just saying you love. Yet another lesson that has also been demonstrated by many of you in ways too many to count this past month.

Over the past couple weeks, each time when I have asked Dr. Estherlyn when she thought I'd be able to go home, she would say *soon*. One day she said, "You know as humans, we all have one thing in common. Lack of patience." Very true. Since her name is Estherlyn, I told her that she had inspired me to re-read that book in the Bible because it's one of my favorites. Esther was a hero because even though she was a queen, she took a huge risk that could have meant instant death for her in order to save the lives of many others. Dr. Estherlyn said she is just one of many strong women in the Bible and asked if I ever noticed that before? I said I guess women have always been strong, courageous fighters and leaders. And she said with this huge smile, "Absolutely!"

Many, many of you have shared with me that my experience has left you speechless, dumbfounded, caught off guard, re-thinking your priorities, and much more. I think that's because this hit really close to home for you. So, here's my verse from Esther that has played over and over in my mind throughout this journey... "And who knows but that you have come to your royal position for such a time as this?" Of course I am not royalty, but I have pondered the question, what does God want me to take away from this happening to me at "such a time as this?"

Anyway, when I do get home, I will still be restricted with visitors and have to be really careful with food not prepared in our own kitchen for a while. Just because of transferring food from one place to the next, not due to your cooking! And absolutely nobody can visit me who hasn't had a flu shot until flu season is over. Apparently, it is rampant this year. My tests have shown that my chances for a recurrence are at a "normal" level. Not perfect but not bad either. I will be seeing a specialist in the next week or so to get a second opinion to confirm my next treatments and any preparations needed should I have a set back down the road. Needless to say, continued prayers for remaining in remission with no infection are still what we need most.

Once again, I reach the end of another lengthy update. I hope you find somewhere in all my rambling the true love and appreciation deep in my heart for every single one of you. We would be lost without you. Tom, Beth, Kate, and I, along with all our family, thank you more than we could ever say.

Stay tuned for updates from home! Hoping you enjoy a relaxing weekend everyone.

Love as always,

Carolee

1/11 Day Thirty-One: Patience

Good morning,

Well, I am sad to say that I am not able to go home today after all. Friends, I am in need of your prayers today on my behalf, if you have time and feel called to do so.

The doctor was fairly certain about me leaving "this weekend" and honestly thought it would be today when she was here yesterday. This morning, the on-call weekend oncologist came in at 8AM and said he was 99% sure I would be going home today and couldn't think of a reason why not either. So, I actually put on regular clothes (thankfully my jeans still fit after all this food I've needed to eat) and waited for the green light.

My kind nurse, Amy came in at 9:15 practically in tears and just shook her head *no*. Here is the reason why. The white blood cells are made up of four main parts. One of them is the Absolute Neutrophil Count (ANC), which is the part that wards off infection. All along, that number had to be greater than 500 or 0.5 of the numbers I've been reporting. Normal white blood counts are 4-7, but we've been waiting for a number above 0.8 for them to be able to break the white blood count down and find the ANC number. Today was supposed to be the day it reached 500. Unfortunately when they ran the test, it is at 45 or 0.04. Obviously a long way off from 500 or 0.5. It may be another day, or two, or three...

The good news is that my white blood count went from 0.6 to 1.0 overnight on Thursday. All my other numbers have been jumping dramatically, too and are where they need to be. If the white count would just take another jump like that, then the ANC number should jump, too. Also, every other thing that should be good is good. I have nothing else wrong with me that would prevent me from going home. I think that is why today was such a surprise to everyone.

This is my prayer request. Please pray that the number jumps today and when they test my blood tomorrow morning at 6AM, the white blood count is closer to 1.8 or even a little more (not a huge jump, because if it goes up dramatically, that's a sign of infection). And more importantly, that the ANC number is greater than 500 in the morning.

My sweet Beth is still asleep and Tom and I are both dreading telling her it may be yet another day, two, three, before I can get home. She is going to be heartbroken. Please pray for peace for all of us as we continue to wait.

I will let you know as soon as I know anything further. In the meantime, I will be praying like crazy. God is good all the time and all the time, God is good. Who knows that there is a bigger reason why I continue to wait. As disappointing as this is, I would rather be sure I will be completely safe from infection or relapse. It's just a little bump in the big road of life anyway.

I'm sure I sound like a broken record, but truly, we have no idea what we would be doing without all of you, our faithful team of cheerleaders! We are going to be throwing one big praise party of gratitude this summer for all of you!

Love as always,

Carolee

1/12 Day Thirty-Two: Getting so close

Good Morning and Happy Sunday,

Since many of you wrote such heartfelt responses to me yesterday - everything from "praying', to "dammit," "hang in there," "tears in my eyes," and "be patient and wait for God's timing which is unknown sometimes, but always best." - I wanted to let you know what happened since I sent the email.

First, within minutes, I could literally feel your prayers. I told my dad recently that I can always feel when people are praying for me. It's happened over the years whenever I have reached out and asked for prayer. I will be anxious, sometimes heart-racing, or a lot of times annoyed or mad at my circumstances. But all of a sudden I am overcome with a feeling of peace that starts at the top of my head, flows right down to my toes and all the unhappy feelings disappear. It's an amazing feeling and I always stop to give thanks for the grace of prayers said and prayers answered.

Then, I had to face Beth trying to hold back tears on FaceTime as I asked her if she was OK. We both burst into tears and I kept telling her it was OK and she said it was not! Eventually, she calmed down and we came up with Plan B. We made a list of junky snacks, Tom actually took her to the grocery store and they arrived mid-afternoon with microwave popcorn, licorice, and 7-Up. Fortunately, the room TV has a VHS player and they have three double sided carts of movies people have donated. There is a huge selection of oldies, westerns, James Bond and lots from the 1980's and 1990's. Beth has enjoyed movies filmed before everyone had computers and cell phones (*Ferris Bueller's Day Off*, *Three Men and a Baby* and *Beverly Hills Cop*, for example). In the end, she slept over with me, which she's done a couple of times in the past and the staff here loves! They treat her like a princess. She is still here today and we are getting ready to watch *Parenthood* with Steve Martin.

We are all much more relaxed and resigned to the fact it may still be some time before I actually do get to go home. Today, the ANC number is at 100, white count at 1.4, red steady at 9.5, and platelets at 186 (normal range is 150-450). The doctor came in this morning and said he would be willing to be flexible with the ANC number needing to be at 500, but it still is too low. That's OK, because as most of you said, "better safe than sorry."

Speaking of platelets, I have failed to properly thank all of you who jumped to the need I had when my number was down to two. My nice friend Rick was wonderful for providing the information needed to know how to go about donating. Friends from Columbus and Chicago who were willing to drive here to donate, if needed. Once again, I was reminded that is what you DO when you love someone. All we ever hear about is to donate blood, but unless you have a cancer or other devastating diagnosis, we would never know of this critical need, too. There was confusion about donating or donating directly to a patient. Here is what I learned...just donate. It has a short shelf life and you don't have to match blood types. It's not necessary to donate to a specific person because they are universal. Plus, you have to get a prescription from the doctor and if they don't use it for that particular patient, it is thrown away. The things I have learned here that I never would have thought twice about previously are endless.

I'm picturing you relaxing over the Sunday paper, attending church, going out for breakfast, running errands, and know some of you are taking kids back to college today. It makes me smile to think about.

My church these days comes from reading. Earlier, I picked up my *Guideposts* magazine and the story was about a schoolteacher from Michigan who had been praying for a husband and family of her own. She was praying that she didn't want to be a 'doubting Thomas' and a verse popped into her mind, Isaiah 49:15-16, "I will not forget you! See, I have engraved you on the palms of my hands." When she opened her daily devotion, it was the same verse. Later that day, her secret prayer partner from Bible study had left an anonymous card in her mailbox with the same verse! It was two years later before she met her future husband. The last line of the story was, "The truth is, I found love before I met my husband, when God reached down and - three times - reminded me I was not forgotten."

What a beautiful thought for this day!

Love to all of you,

Carolee

1/13 Day Thirty-Three: Hoping and praying with you!

Today I had a visitor who is both a client and a minister. He and I have worked together the past several years and he always makes me laugh with his silly singing and joke-telling. We were going over some notes for an upcoming presentation when I thought to ask him, "Have you ever heard God actually speak to you before?" He paused and titled his head to one side. It didn't take long, "No. Have you?" I told him about the several God-whispers in my past. That led to a long discussion about how they probably happen all the time. We humans are all too busy to stop and listen for them. We decided that should be a new practice. Stop and listen. There is a reason for the Bible verse Psalm 46:10 (NIV):

Be still and know that I am God.

1/15 Day Thirty-Five: Dancin'!!!

I'm finally really going home today! So many answered prayers!

1/19 Day Thirty-Nine

Hi everyone,

I can't believe a week has passed already, since I last wrote. It has been a very long week for me. Waiting and watching to make sure it's safe to leave the hospital was extremely stressful on all of us. In the midst of once again spending a night alone, my beautiful friend Amanda sent me the following email last Sunday night:

Today at church the gospel was about loving God, your neighbor and yourself. The priest said a line that really stood out to me. He said God's will is not necessarily our will. Things happen to us in life sometimes to be a conduit for his master plan. I couldn't think of a better example than your situation.

God chose you to teach those around you to have faith in the things we can't control.

God chose you to teach Beth and Tom they are strong on their own but even stronger with you.

God chose you to teach us that even in the face of uncertainty you can chose to accept what is with a smile and a look forward not back.

God chose you because even in the midst of your own fears you reach out and are concerned about others.

God chose me to walk this journey with you.

Once again, that gave me so much hope and reassurance that I spent most of the week walking the halls (I got up to two miles a day), talking to other patient's wives, nurses, techs, etc., and always praying. There were so many stories of people with situations way worse than mine, I could do nothing but offer praise and thanksgiving for my good outcome so far. Also, so many of you have shared your own personal struggles, health issues, on-going cancer battles, and more, that I have filled several pages of my prayer journal just this month. I am blessed to be able to pray for you in return.

I think most of you know that I was finally able to come home from the hospital this past Wednesday. It was 35 days, exactly five weeks, since I had been in our own home. That was the longest time I've ever been away from home and certainly my family.

Even then, it was such a strange feeling to walk in the door. The nurses are very good at making an impression about how easy it is to catch an infection, that once home, I walked around the house with my arms folded across my chest. I was afraid to touch anything or eat anything or practically breathe! I've never been an anxious person, so I was really out of my element with this situation.

After a while, I did calm down and even cooked dinner. Tom and Beth were stunned and protested, but since I love to cook, it made me feel more "normal." As the evening went on, I slowly began to realize that I had made it this far because of my positive attitude, doing everything I was instructed to do, relying on my faith, and the outpouring of love and prayers from all of you. I slept really well that night.

I spent Thursday reading a mountain of material that I had received since I entered the hospital about everything from what is leukemia to how to turn the TV on in the hospital room! Of course, I felt even more normal when I made up file folders for each doctor, insurance claim, type of medicine, hospital facility, etc., and got all of it organized. (I see a bunch of you chuckling and/or shaking your heads.)

In an amazing connection, our church outreach director and her husband put me in touch with a wonderful person at the Leukemia-Lymphoma Society (they had a personal experience themselves and are involved with the organization). The gal there put me in touch with a woman named Joyce at a specialty bone marrow hospital. It turns out she herself had exactly the same diagnosis as me three years ago, is two years younger than me, and is doing fine now. We instantly bonded. As I've said, God is good all the time!

I'm telling you this because we now are fortunate to have second opinion appointments with the heads of the transplant departments at two top cancer hospitals this week. Dr. Estherlyn asked that we see at least one other specialist because she wants to have someone else confirm her recommendations for next steps and let us know every option available for additional treatments. I do have to see her this week as well, to continue tracking my blood cell counts. At some point when my white cells recover, I will need one more bone marrow biopsy to make sure the new cells are normal and leukemia-free. This will probably be the week after this one. By then, we should also have the recommendations of the other doctors and be able to make some decisions.

This is a long, long journey for many years to come. My caring nurse Cathy told me that it's all how you look at life. She said rather than say, "I've never been a sick person," you should say, "I've always been a healthy person." So my new focus is rather than say, "I have leukemia," I will say, "I am recovering from having had leukemia."

For many years, my daily devotional has been *Daily Guideposts*. I didn't take it to the hospital, so when I got home Wednesday, I opened it to December 13th to catch up. Here's the Bible verse from that day: *"Commit everything you do to the Lord. Trust him, and he will help you."* Psalm 37:5 (NIV) Amen!

My precious family and friends, I could never have walked this path, nor continue to walk it, without your love and support. It's a scary road to travel, but I feel I have so many guardians walking it with me that I can't help but smile. Through your prayers, I have reached the hem of Jesus' robe, learned many lessons as did Esther for such a time as this to happen to me, and caught up to Jesus motioning me to follow him closer. I feel him smiling on me and know I will do whatever I can to go where he leads me. I know this because I have been humming the wonderful Easter hymn *He Lives* over and over this past six weeks. Here's part of the chorus in case you're not familiar (*He Lives* was composed in 1933 by Alfred Henry Ackley, 1887-1960):

"He lives, He lives, Christ Jesus lives today!
He walks with me and talks with me
Along life's narrow way....
You ask me how I know He lives:

He lives within my heart."

You are loved and appreciated more than I could ever fully express. Wishing each of you a peaceful week ahead.

Love,

Carolee

1/27 Day 47

Good morning,

I hope this finds you well and staying warm, especially if you live in this arctic blast area of the Midwest-east coast. It is nice to be able to stay indoors as the snow is actually really pretty, since I don't have to go anywhere today.

Being home is the most amazing feeling. Honestly, this past six weeks has never made me more grateful for the simple things in life. I love being here with my family with a few visits from friends. Other than one trip to the grocery store and three doctor appointments, I have not left the house in the past twelve days, which is usually unheard of, if you know my usual schedule.

Many of you have been checking in, so I wanted to update you. (Get ready, this is a long one. Certainly, if you no longer want to receive these updates, please let me know. I'm sure it gets exhausting to read them!) So, last week was a flurry of activity. We started Sunday with our Christmas morning. Tom, Beth and I exchanged gifts, taking our time to just enjoy the simplicity of really looking at each and every one. We had received gifts from near and far and they were all under the tree. So many of you sent wonderful things, we will enjoy them for a long time to come. Thank you once again.

Tuesday, my good friend Janet took me to a follow-up appointment with Dr. Estherlyn. Lots of prayers were answered when I found out my blood counts and platelets had all returned to normal. A very good sign. Consequently, I will be having another bone marrow biopsy January 29th at 8:30AM. This will show if the leukemia cells have returned with my new cells or not. Of course, we are praying that they have not. As always, your prayers for this procedure and good outcome are more than welcome.

On Thursday, we met with the head of bone marrow transplants at University Hospitals. What a wonderful facility, staff, and doctor! We were so impressed with our experience there. The doctor is originally from Argentina and studied/worked at MD Anderson at the University of Texas. MD Anderson is one of the top three hospitals in the country for leukemia research and treatments. He brought much expertise to our area. What I loved is that he said more than once that none of us is God and it is up to Him to decide my outcome in this illness. However, he also said that at this time, he would not recommend a bone marrow transplant.

The next day, we were also blessed to meet with a second specialist at Cleveland Clinic, the director of bone marrow transplants there. While both doctors had different personalities, he also confirmed his recommendation would be to not pursue a bone marrow transplant at this time - praise God!

Let me explain a little about what else they both said. (Fortunately, we have wonderful insurance, so were able to get two second opinions.) They both explained the various treatment options for my type of leukemia. Usually, continued chemo treatments only have a 35% success rate in keeping it in remission. However, I am very fortunate to have a gene that is good enough to bump that percentage up to a 65% success rate with continued chemo. Since the bone marrow transplant also has a 65% success rate (with a 20% fatality rate), they felt the chemo was the way to go at this time.

However, they both also recommended that I be "typed" to get the ball rolling to find a bone marrow donor, in the event I should have a relapse. They explained that a twin is the best match (of course I don't have one) and then full siblings. Even then, siblings are only a match 25% of the time. From there, they have an international database that they compare my DNA to find a suitable match. There is a 70-90% chance of finding a match. The reason the transplant is so dangerous is because the new bone marrow may reject my body, since it's from someone else's body and doesn't recognize mine once transplanted. It's the opposite of an organ transplant where normally the "host" body would reject the organ from someone else.

Many of you have asked if they already put me in remission, why do I need further treatments? We asked this, too. The answer is because as humans, we can only tolerate so much chemotherapy. They know that it will come back without some kind of further treatment, as there was no way to kill every leukemia cell the first time around. Dr. Estherlyn said it's like washing it out of our bodies. I said I thought it sounds like when you run vinegar through your coffee maker, followed by three pots of water. She laughed and agreed with my description.

What an education! If you're still reading along, I am sure you, like me, have learned more about leukemia and the medical field than you ever wanted to know! Tuesday, I came home so upbeat, Thursday, not so much. The percentages of survival, staying in remission, etc., are more than scary. By Friday, I felt better, but by Saturday night, I was sad again. Everyone keeps commenting on my positive attitude, but I feel like someone who has experienced the death of someone close. It's a roller-coaster ride of emotions. My old, carefree life has died and I live daily with the knowledge that this might all come to an end way sooner than I ever wanted.

I have said quite a few times lately that I'm really not as nice as everyone thinks I am and I'm not sure why everyone is being so wonderful to me. I can be really judgmental, a huge gossip, impatient, and lack flexibility in my ways. I have made plenty of mistakes in my life, too. And, even though I was raised a traditional Presbyterian, it wasn't until my mid-thirties that I really longed to know Christ and learn about the true meaning of being a Christ follower. It really sunk in when I studied *The Purpose Driven Life* and then started attending Bible studies by Beth Moore when I was in my late thirties. If you've never done either, and are interested in learning more, try it - life changing for sure. Although I'm not afraid of dying, I just want to learn more, do more, and love more before I go.

I finally reminded myself that when I was first diagnosed, I was told the survival rate of leukemia is 70%, but I was also told to throw that number away. The 70% takes into account older people, people with many health problems, people who have smoked and/or taken drugs, were alcoholics, or worked around chemicals their whole lives. None of these things applied to me. I immediately bumped that number up to 90% in my mind after hearing that. So, if I now look at the 65%, I should also take into account these things. I am choosing to focus on being one of the 65-90% who survive.

I did ask both doctors what their opinions were on the idea that I've been told if you survive leukemia for two years, it usually doesn't come back and that it never comes back after five years. Both said that most relapses occur within the first year and both agreed that it is extremely rare to come back after three years. I asked when that timeline begins and was told it's when I was first diagnosed. This sensible specialist said, "Count each thing you get through as a positive milestone. You already came through the first round of chemo with little problems. That's the first one. Keep counting every positive thing as another milestone. And whatever you do, listen to just one 'quarterback.' You have one of the best in Dr. Estherlyn."

The other doctor put it this way, "Once again, we are not God. You can never say it won't come back, but nobody can say they will never get cancer or any other life threatening disease. Nobody does anything to do this to themselves. You can't tell me an 18 month old baby who is diagnosed with this did anything in their life to bring on leukemia." I said, "Nor did their parents" and he said, "Exactly. It just happens. Go live your life, stay active and keep a normal routine. That's the best advice I can give you." When we parted, he walked out the door, looked back and said with a smile, "I hope I never see you again." That brought my spirits back up, because he meant that he never wanted me to have a relapse or need a transplant.

And, so I pray. I pray for peace, calm, continued remission, not letting the enemy win by worrying or being sad, a good outcome from the biopsy this week, ease in tolerating the continued chemo treatments, no infections, never needing a bone marrow transplant, seeing my beautiful Beth grow up and have a family of her own one day, watching our darling grandson grow up and live a great life as an adult, and so much more. I pray for you, giving thanks for an army of prayer warriors, family, friends, and people I don't even know. I pray for your peace, good health, happiness, success, and thanksgiving to God for placing in your heart the desire to pray for me. Nobody has ever been more blessed than me for this gift.

So, here's what's next. I go Wednesday for the bone marrow biopsy. All three doctors said they do not anticipate any new leukemia cell growth because my numbers recovered so well. Also, a lot has to do with the fact that my platelets recovered very well. Wow - remember that prayer request? They went from a low of two and are now at 355 (normal range is 150-450). My sweet Beth said, "Mom, it's NOT coming back. You know why? Because you're you again. You don't have any random bruises, you're not sleeping all the time, and you're smiling again."

If the biopsy comes back clear, I'll start one of three to four more rounds of chemo, probably next Monday. This means five days back at Northeast

Medical Hospital, with chemo twice a day for three hours each for four or five days. Even though it will knock my counts down again, I should be able to come home by Friday night each time, as long as I don't get any infections. When we asked why I could come home immediately, we were told because I'm starting out with healthy cells this time, not unhealthy ones. Even so, I'll have to be very careful to avoid any type of infection for one to two weeks once home each time. We're hoping I can have these treatments the first week of each month, so that by Easter (and if not Easter, then Mother's Day), I will be set in remission for the long haul. And, spring will be here by then, with flowers, sunshine, warmth, and life anew.

I realize this update is super long and I appreciate your interest in all of this information as we continue down my path to recovery. I've said it so much this past couple of months, but it never stops being true. I would not be where I am today without you. Thank you for bringing me joy every step of the way.

Love,

Carolee

2/5 Day Fifty-Six

Happy Wednesday!

It's been about 10 days since I last wrote, so I wanted to catch you up with my progress. Before I do, there are quite a few of you who I would like to acknowledge.

After my last update, which was really 'apprehensive' as my friend Scott put it, once again so many of you jumped right in to cheer me up. Our cancer support church group was especially encouraging by sharing so many of your stories of your own cancer journeys that I was instantly connected and surrounded by your love. It made me realize that this could be so much worse and I am one blessed person to be handling this without huge numbers of other issues that come along with treatments. My heart goes out to all of you with gratitude for sharing your stories.

Then, I had prayers far and wide from 'Team Atlanta,' family and friends from coast to coast, and a couple of friends who live overseas. Wow! I still can not get over the outpouring of love and care from so many. I continue to receive cards, emails, and texts every day from people checking in, asking how to help, sharing stories, and telling me not only that they continue to pray, but also how many prayer groups they have asked to pray for me. This includes all types of religions, too. I have had friends tell me they are praying in synagogues, during special mass services, and churches of all denominations far and wide. Again, just "Wow!"

Additionally, I have to thank all my incredible clients. Thankfully, not one has cancelled a contract and every single one from the beginning has said, 'Just take care of you. We'll keep the ball rolling until you can come back.' I am thankful more than I can say to have the opportunity to work from home at a job I love with people who could not be more inspiring. One of the reasons for my delay in sending this update is because I needed to actually do my part for these clients catching up with missed deadlines.

How grateful I am once again to live in a place that allows me to own my business and work with such wonderful people.

So, long story short (ha!), because of all of you, I picked myself up and decided to get on with my 'new' life where I am overcoming cancer. I was able to visit with some friends while I was home, which was very fun. I even asked my 'birthday girls' to come over and un-decorate our house from Christmas with a two day notice (if you're in any of these girlfriend groups, you know how difficult it is to gather a busy group together unless it's at least a month out). No time like the present is a new way of planning for me. How great it was that four gals showed up on a freezing Monday night, wine and snacks in hand, and filled our living room with love and laughter for the next few hours. My sweet Beth and I were even able to have a mother-daughter day on Saturday, so she could get her Chipotle fix, I could have my Starbucks fix, and we could browse a few winter clearance sales together. I really wanted to go to church Sunday, too, but decided against it, because I wasn't quite sure how to avoid all the hugging everyone would undoubtedly shower me with! (Sadly, I can't be very close to people yet due to flu and cold season running rampant this winter.)

On to my progress...I had my third bone marrow biopsy last Wednesday morning. Dr. Estherlyn said it looked good as she extracted it and once again, she would probably have the preliminary report that afternoon. But by late afternoon, we had not had any results, so I called the doctor's office. Nobody was available to tell us anything about the biopsy results. As usual, fear started to creep in. But once again, my beautiful Bible study gals, our wonderful pastors, and others jumped right in and started praying. Later I found out that I slept like a baby that night, but several others had restless nights. Yes, I had felt your prayers. By mid-morning Thursday, I still had not heard the test results. So many of you texted and e-mailed asking what happened, that I finally called the office again. Dr. Estherlyn picked up the phone and said, "It's good. It's preliminary, but it's good. We'll see you Monday morning." Whew! Relief has a whole new meaning these days.

Once again, our prayers have been answered by no new leukemia growth. I am back at Northeast Medical Hospital this week for chemo treatments, going home Saturday should there be no fever, infections, or other unexpected side effects. So far, so good. I'll be doing this process the first week of March and April, too. When Dr. Estherlyn came in Monday morning, she asked if anyone had called us with the final biopsy report. I said no and she promptly got me a copy. When she handed the three page print-out to me, she said, "It's the best report anyone could have." Can I say WOW one more time? I have said so many times lately that if I survive this, I am going to be the poster child for proof of the power of prayer. You have all saved me time and again already, not just from this illness, but from sadness, fear, and loneliness, too.

As usual, God puts messages right in front of me just when I need them. Here's a few short stories I thought I would share...First, I have been catching up on my daily devotions, so Monday morning I was up to January 15th. You might remember that was the day I came home from the hospital the first time. The message was about a man from New York City who always started longing for spring about mid-January. Spring is when I should be done with all these treatments, so I could definitely relate. The Bible verse was an old favorite that day, Matthew 6:30 (NIV), "And if God cares so wonderfully for flowers that are here today and gone tomorrow, won't He more surely care for you?"

Next, I was watching the *Today Show* with Hoda and Kathie Lee. Hoda had written a book and they had asked viewers to write in about how it had inspired them. They chose two viewers to come in from all the responses they had received. One was a 27-year-old girl who had overcome a devastating illness that actually claimed her life for five full minutes until the doctors saved her. She told how she had read Hoda's book where she talked about being scared. She had been scared for so long, living in fear, she could choose to be weak, but chose instead to be strong and face obstacles head on. Such an inspiration!

(http://www.nbcnews.com/id/36090945?launch=54270164&config=26185044)

Last, if you watch the news, you saw that Pete Seeger passed away last week. I was not aware of his background or his music until all the news stations started reporting about his death. What a wonderful man with an extremely interesting history. I was familiar with the songs *Turn, Turn, Turn, We Will Overcome,* and more made famous by others. But my favorite was the news coverage of him singing, *This Little Light of Mine.* How many of you remember singing that at Sunday School? I guarantee if you think about it, you'll be humming it all day, too.

(http://www.cbsnews.com/news/an-appreciation-of-pete-seeger/)

Once again, we continue to give our thanks to each of you for your constant care, love, and prayers. You were the inspiration for my new year meditation words: Focus, Give, Rejoice!

Love,

Carolee

2/16 Day Sixty-Seven

Hi Everyone,

Here we are on another Sunday night and I felt I should write the latest about my experience with recovery from leukemia. So many of you write to ask for more information, it sometimes takes me awhile to come up with anything newsworthy to tell you! As always, it never stops amazing me that you tell me how much you appreciate the updates, get worried when you don't hear anything, and continue to share your love for me and my family. I love getting so many well wishes and just yesterday received five more cards in the mail. Is it crazy to try to keep saying thank you? It just doesn't seem enough, but is truly filled with every bit of appreciation I have.

So, I came home from my first round of 'consolidation chemo' last Saturday with instructions to take it easy and see the doctor on Monday, which I was happy to do. My counts were still fairly normal, but dropping. I received a shot of a drug to help boost my white count, being told it would take three or four days to work. On Monday night, Beth and I were watching TV when at 9:00 on the dot, I felt a sharp stabbing pain in my left eye. It felt like an eyelash or something had lodged itself under my eyelid. No matter what I tried, it would not go away. I spent Tuesday and Wednesday walking around the house with sunglasses on and the slightest light was extremely painful. However, by Thursday morning, I woke up and it was completely back to normal. I had a follow-up appointment with the doctor that morning and we all decided it was probably a reaction to the eye drops they were giving me during chemo to avoid extreme dryness of the eyes.

Also on Thursday, my numbers had dropped again, but the doctor felt the shot may not yet have taken effect. So back home and more resting and waiting. Then, yesterday, I noticed tiny red dots all over the back of my hands, lower legs, and tops of my feet. This had happened in the hospital after my very first round of chemo and they felt it was a reaction to one of the preventative antibiotics I had been taking. I called and got the weekend doctor who told me it was probably low platelets and if I experienced unusual bleeding, fever, or other flu like symptoms, I was to go to the ER. By 4PM, my gums were bleeding. However my doctor had told me not to go to the ER but call the oncology floor instead. I did that and they promptly told me to come down for platelets. I have to say that the staff at Northeast Medical Hospital make it the best experience every time. Prompt, efficient, and just nice people. I was there and back home in five hours. They even insisted the security guard take me to my car which I could see directly across the street from the main door.

However, I was very shocked to find out during that visit last night that my counts were dangerously low (white blood at 0.4, red at 8.2, platelets at 2... yes all the way back down to two!). Those are the types of things that I start getting really anxious over as that is what can bring on infections and my inability to fight them. So, too tired to write or text all of you, I took to Facebook and asked for prayers. Once again, many, many people immediately came to my rescue and started praying. Although I slept very restlessly, I finally dozed off around 5am and slept the next four hours very soundly. I have done nothing today but sit around on the couch and watch TV. Back to the doctor in the morning and I am sure more platelets.

As my parents reminded me today, it was three to four weeks after my first round of chemo before my counts came back. And the reason I can be home and wait this time is because I started out healthier, I have nothing else wrong physically, and I truly think the doctors feel our home is a more clean environment than a 500 patient hospital. Here's a fun side note, my nurse last night, Laura, was talking to me and left the room. When she came back, she said she just had to tell me that she thought I knew her sister. Turns out her sister Sharon lives right across the street from me and we attend a Bible study together! How small is this world?!

This morning, I had an email from my friend since second grade and she asked if it hurts? I told her that quite honestly, I feel completely fine. It's not until I look in the mirror at my tired face, lack of hair, and thinning body that I remember. I am more tired this week, but that's because my counts are low. Many of you ask if I am getting anxious to be busy again and I said my new busy is getting up by 8AM, talking to friends on the phone, drinking coffee at the kitchen table all morning, and maybe checking my email before noon. If you knew me before this, I was up by 5:45AM every morning, had checked email and Facebook, and finished at least two cups of coffee by 7AM most days. Then, off to multiple meetings, errands, or catching up on work projects till dinner time, off to Beth's activities or other events, and usually sitting down when I fell into bed by 10PM or so! It's funny how fast those things can change and just not be all that important when you are dealt a new hand like I was.

Do I miss it? Sometimes. I missed my favorite time of year in December because it meant missing so much family and friend time together more than anything. Last night, I insisted that rather than sit around the hospital with me for hours on end that Tom and Beth attend a celebration for our good friend's daughter's engagement party. Beth has been my rock since I have been home this past month and definitely deserved some fun. It does make me sad that our social lives have come to a screeching halt. I even found out from Beth that she is not being invited to some of her friend's birthday parties. I told her people get scared when there is a terrible illness like this and maybe they're afraid they would be taking her time away from being with me. As she said, it would have been nice to at least have been invited so she could make the decision to attend or not. My sweet girl is mature beyond her years.

But, my new attitude is that there will be other parties, Beth knows she is loved, spring and summer will be here before we know it, and I have already made it through three months of this illness. If all it takes to survive this is giving up four or five months to live a long life here on earth, then that's just fine. I am a quarter of the way through my first year already, which is when most relapses occur. By the end of these consolidation treatments, I'll be half way there, and since Christmas comes around faster every year, in the blink of an eye, I will be through the first year. Two years beyond that, and I'll be home free, God willing.

So in the meantime, as my wonderful dad said recently, our lives are in God's hands. Anything can happen, any time, for any reason, to any of us. He said to just live every day the best we can because there is no sense in worrying about things we can't control. Amen, Daddy!

That's about it for now. Of course, all of you cheerleaders continue to keep me positive, loved, and just moving forward with a smile always in my heart from gratitude. Your prayers keep me going most of all. You remind me of one of my very favorite things, because you all live your 'dash' the way that I want to by inspiring me to love more in every way possible. Take a moment to read the poem *The Dash* and you will see what I mean.

(http://play.simpletruths.com/movie/the-dash-poem/)

Love,

Carolee

3/4 Day Eighty-Three

Hello Everyone,

What a time I've had the past couple of weeks since I last wrote! Many ups and downs, but always with a grateful heart that you have been with me with your love, care, and unending prayers.

After that last update of eye pain and low platelets, I was finally feeling better. Then, Wham! My red blood count dropped dangerously low and my heart rate soared up to 160 (normal rate is 70-80). Fortunately, I was at the treatment center getting platelets when that happened, so they immediately whisked me to ICC (Intensive Cardiac Care) to put me on meds and give me a blood transfusion. Before I got there, I was able to send a text, crying out for prayers. By the time I reached the ICC, my heart rate had returned to normal. Being Friday night, there was a resident cardiologist and a no-nonsense looking nurse waiting for me. When they read my heart rate, they looked at each other and said, "Now what do we do?" The nurse asked me what happened and I told her my prayer warriors were on it. She said, "Amen!"

So I spent the night listening to monitors beeping, watching lights go off and on, having my blood pressure taken every hour, and not getting any sleep. My heart rate never went above normal and I received two units of red blood.

On Saturday, my sensible nurse from oncology, Karen, came flying into my room asking, "What happened? We saw your name on the computer and we were all worried. I told the nurses I would find out." So, I explained everything, and we had a nice visit. I never stop being thankful for the kind people who care for me at the hospital. So, long story short, I've had a-flutter for nearly nine years when I first experienced thyroid issues. It has been under control with that med, but now the doctors are saying that the chemo, low blood counts, leukemia, etc., could have brought it on again.

They sent me home with a low dose medication. I have to say that I don't ever remember having a reaction to medication until this one. I felt like a weight was being pressed on my sternum, I was light-headed, tired, and so anxious. None of those things are my normal, especially the anxiety. It gave me a whole new appreciation for those who suffer with that disorder. I just did not feel like me and it was very disturbing. Even Beth noticed, saying, "Mom, you were so chill last time you were home, but now you're so anxious." (And I thought I was doing a good job hiding it from her - ha!)

By last Tuesday, I was trying to stay occupied with work projects which I enjoy and am very happy to be able to do, but the anxiety kept creeping in. Finally, I called a pastor friend and asked him to pray with me, which of course he did and of course made me relax. Afterward, several friends called seemingly from out of the blue and made me feel even better. Once again, I was reminded that I am never alone on this journey even at home by myself. As my loving stepmom pointed out, this was the first month of being home and not under the microscopic care of the hospital staff. She said next time home I will know what to expect and not be so anxious. She always seems to know just what I need to hear.

Yesterday, I checked back into the hospital for my second round of consolidation chemo for the leukemia. Dr. Estherlyn is on vacation for two weeks, so her nurse practitioner was making rounds. I told her the whole story about my heart and asked if I could see the cardiologist. She also checked my thyroid and ordered an EKG; both were normal. Later in the afternoon, the cardiologist came in and talked to me, basically saying the medication was such a low dose that it was more a precaution. He said since I would be here this week that I could stop taking the meds and see what happens.

Last night, I fell asleep at 7:30PM and slept most all night. This morning for the first time since the whole 'heart episode' started, I felt calm, rested, and positive again. They did come in and perform an echocardiogram today and I'm waiting for those results. The cardiologist came in and said if it comes back normal, I should be able to stay off meds, but if not, I should plan to take something for life. I asked if there were alternative medications, because I did not want to take the same one. I am more than willing to follow doctors orders, but not at the price of peace of mind! He said there are beta blockers and some other thing that I didn't catch. Whichever one I was taking, he will try the other one, if needed. Of course, during the entire test, I was humming *He Lives (Within My Heart)* which was so calming. We will see what happens from here, but obviously hoping for a good test result.

On to happier things... We were able to have some fun during my nine days when I can be out and about this past week. We had dinner at a favorite local Italian restaurant with two other families last Sunday night and home in time to watch the season finale of *Downton Abbey,* which Beth and I are hooked on. The rest of the week was busy with a work meeting/lunch (bonus, these ladies are some of the best prayer warriors around and just plain nice people), did mundane things like sign our taxes, pay bills, clean house, laundry and grocery shopping. Cable station TCM made my week by playing *Casablanca* one night, so I was able to watch my all-time favorite classic movie. Beth and I had our monthly mother-daughter day of lunch out and shopping, which is always a highlight. Then a couple hours of the Oscars. FaceTime with Kate and adorable James rounded out my 'good' week.

Now, I am spending the week once again at Northeast Medical Hospital receiving chemo. So far, so good. Sometimes I think these extra things that keep happening to me are so I will actually learn new lessons. Like not to be complacent, expecting everything will be just fine and going back to 'normal.' I have learned there is no such thing as normal and without daily prayer and meditation, the unexpected will come knocking to remind me where my focus should be. I found this great website some time ago: BibleGateway.com. There is even an app for your tablet and phone. You can type any verse, phrase, word, etc. in the search bar and it will produce every instance of it in the Bible. Such a helpful resource. Through all my research and prayer time, I have really come to realize that my place in this world is to be a care giver. I always thought that before, but this experience is teaching me how. I believed by fundraising, sending cards, making meals, and offering to help that I was doing the best I could. Even though I will still do those things, I will do them with a heart filled with prayers and patience, by listening more, and loving fully. I cannot wait to be recovered completely, so I am ready to help when called.

In the meantime, we have spring break to look forward to later this month. Kate and her family will be visiting us all week. We have a 'celebrate family' party planned at my in-laws while they are here to celebrate lots of family birthdays in March, so the Ohio family can finally meet baby James, and just be together. The weather forecast predicts 40's and 50's that week, but we Ohioans know how that goes! Either way, spring will arrive at some point, the grass will grow and flowers will bloom, birds will chirp, and little animals will scurry around the trees. The sun will shine its warmth on us all and this long, cold winter will become a distant memory.

There was a post I read on Facebook last week: "The 9 Essential Habits Of Mentally Strong People" (http://huff.to/1fdpJgK)

As I read it, I was once again reminded of how very blessed I am to have each of you loving, caring, and praying for me and my family. You are strong in so many wonderful ways and appreciated every day. Thank You!

Love,

Carolee

3/30 Day One Hundred Nine

Happy Sunday!

I cannot believe it's been nearly four weeks since I last wrote to all of you. Time continues to march on with ups and downs, but always with gratitude for the gift of waking up to a new day. It's been three and a half months since my diagnosis. I truly sound like a broken record, but want you to know that I would not be here today without the love and care each of you continues to give.

How do I know? Because I received the most special gift on Friday. I had no idea that my beautiful Kate had sent you an email asking for special pictures and notes for her to create a memory book for me. I knew I was going to burst into tears as soon as I started reading it, but actually, I was smiling most all the way through. You are all amazing as the love just poured out through your messages and photos. I could not be more thankful for this wonderful gift.

I also want you to know that I have kept every single e-mail and card that you have sent throughout this time and will continue to do so. One of my projects has been to copy all the e-mails into a single document. I haven't made a lot of progress yet. Even though I have most of the December notes done, I still have 430 e-mails to save! Please keep them coming whenever you have time and feel like doing so. They mean the world to me.

After I wrote on March 4th, I had an interesting visit from a hospital volunteer named Melanie. This curly dark haired 40-something gal popped her head in my hospital room and asked if I would mind the visit. She told me she was a patient of Dr. Estherlyn as well, and had survived stage four breast cancer. Since she had done so well, she wanted to "pay it forward" by coming back and visiting patients going through treatments to provide encouragement. What a joy Melanie was. Here's the interesting part. She hesitantly told me that she is a believer and waited for my reaction. I told her that was wonderful and I was sure her faith had sustained her through everything, just like me. Melanie asked me if I thought Dr. Estherlyn is a Christian or not. Melanie said she was hesitant to send her a Christmas card, wondering if she was Jewish, or if she would be offended by the card.

I shared with Melanie the time that I told Dr. Estherlyn that Esther was one of my favorite books of the Bible and how Dr. Estherlyn replied that I should look up some other strong women in the Bible, like Ruth. Melanie stopped at that point and asked if she could show me something? Out of her bag came a journal with a quote. She said, "I just went to a women's retreat and the message was from Esther... wait for it... *"And who knows but that you have come to your (royal) position for such a time as this?"* Thank you, God, for once again reminding me that you are ever present in this time.

So I continued to walk the halls a couple of times that week. As usual, I always try to find a new song to hum. I was envisioning my hand in Jesus' hand, walking along a path and praying that I would follow wherever He led. Suddenly the song, *Put Your Hand in the Hand* popped into my mind. "Put your hand in the hand of the man who stilled the water, Put your hand in the hand of the man who calmed the sea, Take a look at yourself and you can look at others differently, By puttin' your hand in the hand of the man from Galilee." ("Put Your Hand in the Hand" was composed by Gene MacLellan, 1938-1995)

Here's another fun story from that week. Since my heart issue was still so up in the air, the doctor ordered an EKG and echocardiogram. Fortunately, they both came back normal. The cardiologist decided my elevated heart rate the week before had come from dehydration and extreme anemia. While he was showing me the ultrasound and pointing out how the heart works, I said, "Look at that! There are four little heart shapes, just like when you draw them." He gave me the funniest look and said, "Yes, those are the chambers." He probably thought I was crazy, but usually, you just see a picture of the whole heart and I could never figure out why people draw hearts the way they do! He finished the visit by telling me he didn't need to see me again. I ended that week with an extra red blood transfusion, just to be on the safe side.

The next two weeks were filled with many visits to the doctor for blood and platelet infusions. Even though I got an all clear from the cardiologist, I think I have developed "white coat syndrome" because as soon as I walk into the doctor's office, my heart starts racing. I can rationalize all of this because my entire life I have had low blood pressure and the thought of having heart issues, not to mention a night in the hospital ICC, completely set me over the edge. How strange that the leukemia has never had that effect on me! Once again, I started texting my prayer warriors to get me calmed down and the two weeks went by fairly uneventful. Even though I was shocked that my platelets were at zero twice that first week home, which brought on awful mouth sores again, I was relieved to receive transfusions and put that behind me. Fortunately, my white counts recovered, along with the red blood and that did not cause any issues. I did find out that since I have had so many blood transfusions, my antibodies have changed, making it much more difficult for them to locate the red blood that I need. Another thing to pray about.

Sadly, we experienced a huge disappointment. We had so been looking forward to Kate and her family visiting us for Beth's spring break from school this past week. We had lots of plans made with family and friends.

However, there was a mechanical failure with their plane out of Seattle and after five hours at the airport with a baby, they called it quits and went home. There simply were no other flights out until late Sunday since everything was sold out due to spring break. After a day or so, we all decided summer would be a better time for them to visit, when I will be past treatments, the weather will be better, and we can do more things outdoors together.

We did fill the week with other things. Beth had friends over, we went shopping and out to lunch, a fun trip to try on wigs (!), and a quick trip to Columbus to visit my parents and celebrate some special family birthdays together. I was also able to share two milestones with Beth these past few weeks as she took her driving test, got her license, and went on an interview in hopes of getting hired for her first job.

One of the things I have been trying this month is spending time in meditation as I pray and read my devotions. It's interesting that when you pray and your mind starts to wonder that if you stop and focus on breathing that your attention is restored and things become more clear. Maybe because this is the Lenten season, everything I have been reading seems to be sending the same message: Focus! Our church Lenten devotional is titled "Change Your Focus" and most of the other things I have been reading mention in one form or another, "Where is your focus?" I hear your, Lord!

So, why am I still so anxious as I pack my yoga pants, walking shoes, and other essentials for my last week of consolidation chemo that starts tomorrow morning? I think that since I have taken this journey one step at a time, only allowed myself to contemplate just so far into the future, and been in "pause" mode since mid-December, the anxiety comes from wanting more time now more than ever. The "what-if's" creep in like what if I have a relapse, what if my heart fails, what if I get an infection, etc., etc. ??? I love my family, friends, home, and life here so much that I just don't want to go back to Northeast Medical Hospital. But, I will. And through the grace of God, the love and prayers from all of you, and re-focusing on the dawn of each new day, I will be fine.

My new vision is walking into our beautiful church on Easter morning and feeling the absolute joy that comes with the celebration that Christ is risen, He is risen indeed. And with that gift, my life can once again move forward.

With all my love and appreciation,

Carolee

P.S. I looked up Ruth in The Bible as Dr. Estherlyn suggested:

"But Ruth replied, "Don't urge me to leave you or to turn back from you.

Where you go I will go, and where you stay I will stay.

Your people will be my people and your God my God."

"Boaz replied, "I've been told all about what you have done for your mother-in-law since the death of your husband—how you left your father and mother and your homeland and came to live with a people you did not know before. May the Lord repay you for what you have done.

May you be richly rewarded by the Lord, the God of Israel, under whose wings you have come to take refuge."

Ruth 1:16, 2:11-12, The Bible (NIV)

5/4 Day One Hundred Forty-Three

Happy May!

Even though spring has been a long time coming here in Northern Ohio, we have received glimpses here and there. As I'm writing this, the sun is peeking out from the clouds and the daffodils are swaying in the spring breeze. Once again, I am reminded just how fast time moves along. It's been five weeks since I last wrote! Lots of news to share since then, too.

I did go through my last week of chemo the week of March 31st and it was several weeks of recovery after. It's very true that the more chemo you receive, the harder it is for your body to recover. After a total of 28 doses of chemo over almost a four-month period, I needed eight platelet transfusions and two red blood transfusions to recover from this last round. Thankfully, my girlfriends were quick to answer when I would text, "Who wants to go with me this afternoon for a transfusion?" What a blessing to have that time together, when normally I would have been busy running from one thing to the next instead of sharing quality time laughing and talking. Even the nurses at the treatment center commented that we were having way too much fun! Finally, most all the side effects wore off and my counts recovered. As usual, I relied on prayers from so many of you to carry me through and of course, they did.

That last week in the hospital was actually somewhat uplifting. I took my very special memory book that Kate had made and so many of you contributed to with your thoughts and pictures. Anyone and everyone who walked into my room took a look at it. The word spread and I had nurses, techs, and visitors asking to see it! Fortunately, I was able to go home Friday night that week instead of my usual Saturday morning. As I finished up my last round of chemo that evening, there was a knock on my door. In walked four of the nurses and techs with a flower bouquet surrounded by balloons made from their plastic gloves! Each glove balloon had a face or a message drawn on them. They also gave me a "happy last chemo" card that was signed by every staff member on the floor! They must have worked on it all week, because I hadn't seen some of the people since the beginning of that week. The staff ushered us out with smiles and hugs and, "Come back and see us, but not to stay," as we left later that night. It was incredible and I feel like I left part of my family behind.

As always, I spent a lot of time this past month reading inspiring messages. And, as usual, there seemed to be a common thread in everything I found. The word this month: Hope. I actually started seeing this in places throughout my experience and even before. Some time ago, when Beth was much younger, one of my best friends was named Hope. As so often happens, friendships come and go and we have since lost track of that friendship. Then, when Beth was a little older, I attended a Bible study named Hope. Our theme verse was Romans 15:13 (NIV), "May the God of hope fill you with all joy and peace as you trust in him, so that you may overflow with hope by the power of the Holy Spirit." When I came home from my initial five weeks at the hospital, a mound of gifts was waiting for me under our still decorated Christmas tree. One of those gifts was from one of the first friends I made when we moved from Columbus. It was a soft pink blanket with this same Bible verse embroidered on it. Then, just before I went in the hospital for my last treatment, a good friend brought by a small gift box and left it for me in our mailbox. Inside was a beautiful charm with a cross, a dove, and the word Hope inscribed on it. She also gave me a daily affirmations booklet, which has been wonderful to read, DailyWord.com.

The best part of this month was walking into church on Easter Sunday and being completely overwhelmed with joy. As the organ started and the brass band began to play, I got chills from the beauty of it all. How appropriate the sermon was titled, "Unstoppable." Even though Jesus came for nothing other than to love us and show us how to love each other, humans still took his life in a terribly cruel manner. Even though they placed him in a tomb and rolled a huge boulder in front of it to seal him in, He was unstoppable. Even though they tried to take him away for good, there was no stopping his power. Jesus' love for us is definitely unstoppable.

How do I know? Because when I went to see Dr. Estherlyn this past Monday, she removed the "pic line" for chemo and transfusions from my arm. Then she said, "You are in remission. I don't need to see you for a month. Go. Live." And with a huge smile on her face, she gave me a giant hug.

This week has been filled with lots more smiles and hugs, meetings and coffee breaks, shopping. and Bible study. And once again, my Esther Bible story came full circle. Right from the start and even long ago, Esther became one of my very favorite books of the Bible for lots of reasons. My mother's great-grandmother's name was Esther, which made me study the book of Esther in the Bible - twice actually. When I was diagnosed with leukemia, the oncologist recommended to me was named Estherlyn. Not knowing anyone else in the field, I commented, "Sure. I like the name Esther." Dr. Estherlyn walked in and took charge of my treatment and recovery. Then, Melanie, the hospital volunteer, came into my room that March evening and showed me her retreat theme, straight from the book of Esther. And, just this week, I was at a business breakfast and a beautiful woman commented on a situation another person was perplexed in how to handle. Her comment, "*You were put in this position for such a time as this.*" (Esther 4:14, NIV)

So why is this verse from Esther so important to me? Because Esther took a chance. And I admire her for that because if you know me, I am not a risk taker, adrenaline junkie, or dare devil. I have no desire to go to outer space, bungee jump, climb Mt. Everest, or skydive! Maybe Esther wasn't an adrenaline junkie either. But, when given a choice, instead of staying quiet and saving herself, Esther risked her own life and saved the lives of an entire population.

I think my risk in all of this has been to put this faith journey out there in such a bold manner. That's not anything I would normally do. I'm not comfortable quoting Bible verses or telling stories about God, creation, mankind, and Jesus. I know many other people who could do this confidently and without hesitation. I told a story to a pastor friend at the beginning of my diagnosis as to why I think this happened to me. I told him I had been praying for some people to get to know Jesus. *I kept hearing that little voice saying back, "That's why they have you."*

Every time I think I should stop writing these very long-winded updates, I get e-mails from people I had no idea were even reading them with comments like, "keep 'em coming," "you've changed how I look at things," "I have re-evaluated my priorities and values," "my faith has been renewed," and "thank you for being the voice of God." Wow! Maybe that little voice really was not my own whispering back to me, because I am not that good of a communicator. But God is. Every single one of your cards, box of cookies, e-mails, visits, text messages, gifts, meals, phone calls, and prayers have shown me the truth in this.

It is a long road to a full restoration to life without leukemia. Three to five years to be exact. But, I am choosing to focus on hope. I am blessed beyond words to be surrounded by people willing to share their own stories of hope, inspiring me to stay strong and not look back. I am doing everything I can to make up for this long, long winter. I am revitalizing my company that I love, but more importantly, I am spending more time with family and friends first. As I said to someone the other day, "Deadlines aren't important; people are." And, don't think I'm ending this without another song in my heart! Beth and I were driving last month and singing at the top of our voices *Everything is Beautiful*. Yes, you are!

With So Much Love and Appreciation,

Carolee

<u>6/22 Day One Hundred Ninety-Two</u>

Hello & Happy Summer!

It's hard to believe that seven weeks have passed since I last wrote. It amazes me how fast I wiped my calendar clean last December and how fast it filled back up this past month. So many of you are kind enough to write, text, call, and ask me in person how I am feeling, that I want to give you another update. (Get ready, it's a long one!)

One of my friends recently made the comment that it just feels like cancer is imploding all around us. So, I thought I'd answer one of the most common questions I am asked: Just what were the signs that I was ill? I think I really had this coming on since early November, if not sooner. I had a sinus infection with lots of sinus drainage and watery eyes since late October. Then, I started noticing strange bruises appearing on my hips, legs, and arms - one would appear, disappear, and another would show up somewhere else. Next, I was getting sores on my tongue and inside of my mouth. The only thing I would eat were loaded baked potatoes, but I kept losing weight anyway! And, I was so tired. I would fall asleep right after dinner and sleep all night. I thought I had a 24-hour bug the week before Thanksgiving and spent two days laying on the couch. I rebounded from that and we hosted Thanksgiving (actually four days that weekend with family and lots of great memories). We also had two different Sweet 16 birthday parties for Beth during that time - one for family in Columbus and one with her friends here at home. I was really busy with work, not to mention getting ready for Christmas and all the events that go along with that. The day that I was diagnosed, I had just finished running the sweeper and was decorating the Christmas tree, preparing for our annual Christmas party the next evening. About 2PM that Thursday afternoon, my doctor's office called and said to come in immediately.

You could have knocked me over with a feather when she walked in and immediately said, "You have leukemia. You need to get to the hospital right away." I did ask how she knew and she showed me my blood results. What an education regarding those counts that I have had ever since. (Most of you, too, if you've been reading these!) The bruises and mouth sores came from low platelets. The exhaustion came from low red blood counts. My white blood counts had gone crazy, trying to fight off the leukemia, so those numbers were super high. All were the indicators. Honestly, I thought I was anemic or just needed some vitamins!

I spent so much time these past months looking, waiting, and wondering about what was next. I felt like I was holding my breath all the time. I wouldn't buy anything for myself. I spent a lot of time reading and finally learned to meditate and give yoga another try. What a difference that makes. I should have done that a long time ago. I feel like I just had a relaxing massage every time I leave the yoga studio now. It really is a workout and I am only taking the slow, stretching, meditation class. I also had lots of time to reorganize our house and de-clutter. I found a Bible that had a thick layer of dust on it. It's one of those "Read the Bible in a Year" versions. I opened it and found the bookmarker at January 6th. I have no idea what year that was! So, on May 1st, I started reading the January 1st pages. We'll see how far I get this time!

I was diagnosed with Acute Myeloid Leukemia (M4) on December 12th, more than six months ago. How very blessed I am to be here now, able to let you know that when I had my blood work done the day after Memorial Day, Dr. Estherlyn handed me the report and said, "It's all normal. I'll see you in three months." Wow! I felt like that commercial when the announcer says to the football player, "You just won the Super Bowl. Now what are you going to do?" Why, go to Disney World of course! We actually are going next month. My wonderful parents have a beautiful condo there and it is our home base to all fun Florida excursions. On a side note, did you ever read my book recommendation from January, *Love Does* by Bob Goff? There is a chapter in it about his "office" at Tom Sawyer Island at Disneyland. It's one of those attractions at Disney World that we never seem to take time to visit. After his description, we are going to find it this summer.

It has been just fantastic to be back out and about. I get to actually see so many of you in person now. I continue to be humbled by your words: "I pray for you every day," "My parents pray for you every day and you couldn't ask for better people to pray," "You look so good," "Your coloring is beautiful," and "Is that your real hair?!"

This is a common question. No, it's not actually my real hair. When I was first diagnosed, a nurse told me one of the most psychologically devastating side affects would be losing my hair. Honestly, I find it fascinating. Maybe because I never did lose all my hair, but actually had the same bald spot my grandpa had - the ring of hair around the bald top of your head style.

Thankfully, one of my best friends (another cancer survivor) taught me all about what to do with my fake hair. I have to say, it is the easiest thing - just brush it and go. And, it adds at least 15 minutes to my morning routine. No longer do I spend too much time trying to style my poker straight, thick hair just to walk outside and have it go flat in the humidity. My hair is growing back and it does have some wave. Now, I look like my other grandpa - gray with waves at the very ends. Kate said it looks like Julie Andrews from *The Sound of Music*. Beth was laughing at me, because the other day I took a ruler and tried to measure how long it is. It looks like baby hair and is really soft. Lots of people have said they would get something really different. But, it had been so long since I saw myself looking back in the mirror, I just wanted it to look like my real hair. I was impressed when one of my oldest friends (in length of friendship, not years) asked me recently, "So, is that your own hair?"

It stopped me in my tracks on a couple of occasions when several different friends commented, "I wasn't here for you enough. I want to be a better friend to you now." And comments when they would share experiences with me by prefacing them with, "But it's not as bad as what happened to you." I can definitely say that is not true in the least. Prayers alone were a huge part of all of you being there for me and how you continue to do so. To think that people pray every day for me is too hard to imagine. I would like to think I pray for certain people every day, but I know there are days here and there that I don't. More so, no tragedy anyone experiences is any better or worse than another's experience. Once again, it's the lessons we choose to learn from these situations that define who we become. Some of the best comments I hear (and have ever since I was diagnosed) are from several of you who with all confidence in the world, look at me and say, "I never doubted you would beat this. I knew all along you would be fine." Thank you, thank you! Most of all this past couple of months, I have enjoyed seeing all your beautiful smiles and feeling your warm hugs once again.

So, what have I been doing? Lots of girlfriend time! Spending time with my Columbus family, who I missed so much over the winter. Getting back to work with wonderful clients who never once doubted I would complete my assignments for them. Like I said, de-cluttering our house, which sick or not, somehow always needs done every spring.

I also said good-bye to someone very special since I last wrote. It was with huge sadness that my dear friend Ann lost her 11-year battle with cancer. The lessons learned from her through our entire friendship will live on as long as I am here. I got to spend time with her the day before she passed on and I told her to find our other treasured friend, Grace and have a big party in Heaven. I also asked her to watch out for all of us here and look for us when our time comes. It was timely that the next weekend, our church minister preached about the "cloud of witnesses" or people who go on to life eternal before us and watch over us.

If these two women alone are my cloud of witnesses, I could not ask for more. But, it wasn't long after Ann passed on that I started remembering another spring long ago. My mother had just passed away. I remember planning her funeral and trying to select some music to play. Thankfully, our minister had given me a list of hymns and Bible passages appropriate for funerals. *On Eagles Wings* was one of the hymns. iTunes was foreign to us at that time and I remember Beth helping me as we spent a couple of hours on my computer one night trying to find just the right version of this song. They were either too fast, too slow, too "opera-like," too sad, ...just not right. Then, we found one.

Shortly after my mother left our lives, our beautiful May passed away. May was an older lady from our church who was Beth's babysitter-nanny-adopted Grandma since she was an infant. Within another few months, my dear sister-in-law lost her dad suddenly and her mother shortly after. Every service kept including, *On Eagles Wings* and by the time we got to that last funeral, I could not stop sobbing. (Stay with me - there is a point to this.)

Just after Mother's Day this year, I found my CD and played *On Eagles Wings* once again. As I listened to the words, I started wondering why this is a funeral song? I realize the lyrics are talking about life eternal and that is associated with death. But it also speaks of the promises we have here on earth that we are all under the protection of a mighty God who will never let us down. There is hope in every situation and we will all be together again someday. It left me happy in all the special moments I experienced with every one of these people, knowing they are watching out for me from beyond. Ask yourself who your "cloud of witnesses" are sometime. I hope it makes you smile, too.

There's another song that I keep hearing on the radio around here lately, *Live Like You're Dying* by Tim McGraw. http://www.youtube.com/watch?v=_9TShlMkQnc

I can't begin to tell you how true his words are in this song. Some of my cancer survivor friends have told me it takes about two years to get past the constant thought in the back of your mind that it could come back. It's about that time that you start living like you used to before being diagnosed. I really don't think about it a lot, but it is always something that is just there. I do hope for it to go away for good someday and I still need to stay in remission for a few more years for that to happen. However, I also hope never to lose the absolute truth in the message of this song.

In the meantime, I had a meeting recently with a business associate who I had met with last October. We had put our collaboration on hold due to my diagnosis. When we finally had the opportunity to meet again, she started telling me about a retreat she is planning for August. The theme is "Mind-Body-Spirit" and she has speakers lined up for the mind and body portion. She then explained that she has a well-known doctor who would like to be her speaker for the spirit portion, but she kept feeling like God did not want her to confirm with him. She kept praying and praying that the right person with just the right message would come along. At this point, I began to tell her about these updates and my prayers to find a way to share my story of prayers answered (she has never received these updates). She looked at me with a huge smile and said, "Well, here we are. You're my speaker." I said, "I won't have the draw that this man would have." She replied, "That doesn't matter. God will take care of it." Wow! Yes, prayer works!

And, finally, I took the time to do something that I thought of a while ago. I gathered every card received from so many of you since my diagnosis and laid them out on our living room floor. Then, I went upstairs to the loft and took a picture. 217 cards make a beautiful sight. Just like all of you in my life. Thankful is too small a word to describe how I feel. You are so very loved and appreciated.

Happy summer everyone!

Love,

Carolee

11/17 Day Three Hundred Forty

Hi Everyone,

I know it has been months since you last heard from me. Life is good and I am so grateful to be healthy and happy and still here. Thank you all for your continued prayers for me. I go back for my next three-month check up with Dr. Estherlyn on November 24th and believe me, I will be more than thankful that Thursday as we celebrate Thanksgiving.

It is amazing and a little scary that the holiday season is nearly upon us. December 12th marks the one-year anniversary of my leukemia diagnosis. I hear that if it is coming back, it's usually in the first year, which starts the day of diagnosis. So, my eyes are set on Christmas, our eternal hope in human form!

Happy Thanksgiving!

Love,

Carolee

"Do not be afraid, nor be dismayed, for the Lord your God is with you wherever you go."

Joshua 1:9 (NIV)

When I had to wait two weeks to learn if I would live or die, this is the truth I came to know. And every day since, the decisions I have had to make in order to change my life for the better have been a constant reminder of this.

Chapter Three

Now What?

Wow! That was about all I could think once I finished reading Carolee's dairy. I just looked at her and wondered aloud what she did next. She continued to surprise me with how she went on with her life, as she made decisions and continued to listen for her God-whispers.

All the things you read about a caregiver needing care is more than true. I had gone through this with my mother for years and knew firsthand what it was like to worry and care, all while attempting to maintain a "normal" life.

It's staggering how many marriages fall apart following a health crisis. Mine was one of them. Unfortunately, the numbers of marriages that don't last are even worse for women who had cancer than men.

Was the end of my marriage because this was the icing on the cake following years of turmoil? Was it the excuse that was needed? Was it fear of the unknown? Was it just plain giving up? I can't answer those questions for him, but for me it was a chance to finally stop living a double life of unhappiness while wishing for one of peace. It took a long time to reach that conclusion, even during my recovery and many attempts to try to feel otherwise. I was so sad to think I was going to break another vow. Especially one I made in all good faith, promising God so many years before that I would not break this one.

What's interesting is that I would have this conversation with others who I trusted; none of who knew each other. I kept saying that I should find a way to hold my marriage together regardless of the circumstances. A minister and two doctors all made the same comment, "God doesn't want you to be unhappy." A good friend put it this way when I shared my feelings that this must be God's way of keeping me from leaving my husband. She said, "I think you are looking at this backwards. Maybe instead of God keeping you in this marriage, He is trying to make you ask yourself what else He needs to do before you will leave?"

What happened to us? Well, that's another story for another time. But let me say that you never really know what goes on behind closed doors. As my baby girl has often said, we got really good at playing "happy family" for the outside world. So all those quotes you see on social media about not knowing what someone is going through is definitely the truth.

Just be kind.

Smile.

Give an encouraging word to all those you encounter.

You never know if anyone is really just playing happy at life, too.

I love listening to women I know talk about how they would react if anything ever happened to "me and (fill in the blank)." It's just like any situation that you haven't ever had to experience but think you know exactly what you would do. One of my most thoughtful girlfriends explained it best while we were sharing life experiences over a glass of wine one night. "The way I see it," she said, "there are three types of married couples by the time they have reached this point in life." (Meaning near to empty nesters) "One. They are still very happily married and enjoying life together. Going out, traveling, sitting on their decks enjoying a sunset. You know. We know some of them." Then she told me about the other two types of couples. "Then there are the couples who are living in the same house but living parallel lives. They are really just roommates. We probably know more of these than any other type." (Sad, but true.) "And last, there are the couples who just throw in the towel and say they aren't interested in pretending any longer." I have to tell you that I completely agree.

The funny thing is, the last thing she said was, "Then there is us." You see one of the reasons she and I share a 20-plus year friendship is because we experienced very similar marriages. Neither of us wanted to break a vow or throw in the towel. We wanted so much to be satisfied by staying married the rest of our lives. Unfortunately, our husbands had other behaviors that kept that from happening.

Ironically, as much as my husband said my leaving was the worst thing that ever happened to him, he never changed his behavior toward me. For years, every time I pleaded for him to change, he would pacify me by taking steps toward a peaceful life. But, as soon as I got used to that (which wasn't very long), the old behaviors returned and we were back to square one.

Then I was diagnosed with leukemia. And I thought, well this is certainly God's way of bringing us closer together. That was my hope at least. Unfortunately, it was the exact opposite. My husband claimed that he couldn't help himself because he was afraid of losing me. In the end, he did anyway.

My oncologist kept asking me how I was doing after the many days in the hospital turned into weeks. I couldn't answer that I was afraid because I would die of cancer. I was afraid because I didn't want to leave my daughter with her father. So I prayed, and through those answered prayers, I found the determination to get better because I knew what I had to do once I was healed.

The worst thing was that it took a few months to have enough of my strength back to make a change. But that's not what was hard. I had lived this life for so many years anyway. What forced the issue was when I watched my daughter spiral into a dark place of despair. Beth literally became paralyzed. After many physical tests, she was diagnosed with a form of post traumatic stress disorder. And not because of my illness, but because of what she had to endure while I lived in the hospital those 35 days. That was the icing on the cake for me.

I had no idea if I was going to survive, but I was determined to make a better life for the two of us regardless of how much time I had left on this earth. It took me several months to find a home where I felt we could be safe. Underneath it all, her father knew she had to get out from under his roof as much as I did. Fortunately, our leaving was not a battle I had to fight.

To this day, he hasn't changed his behavior toward me, nor his daughters really. I have studied a lot about why that is. I look at family history and try to make sense of it. Sometimes I think it always came down to money being the most important thing to him. And cancer is not inexpensive. Neither are children. So, was it really just a fear that I could get sick again and at what cost? The realization that college expense, a wedding, and more grandchildren would eventually come along; all with a price tag attached? Or was it the other behaviors that took over him being reasonable? Was it me? Was it the burden of a family? I stopped asking these questions a long time ago.

Then I found out through mutual friends that he told them I left him because the chemo had changed me. I had the opportunity to say this to him not long after I heard this, "You're right. The chemo did change me. It made me stronger and it made me realize that life is short. I am in charge of my own happiness. And that you don't get to be!"

My ex-husband used to ask me why I couldn't forgive him for the way he had treated me. I would always answer, "There is nothing to forgive. It's just who you are." And he would ask, "Don't you know that I love you?" To which I would answer, "I know you love me in the only way you know how." After much counseling, studying, meditating, yoga, and prayer, I came to realize that what I really needed to do was to find a way to forgive myself. Forgiveness for putting myself and my daughters into a relationship that was so very unhealthy. Then, find forgiveness for staying in it for so very long.

This will probably make no sense, but one day I was at church and the message was about forgiveness. We watched a video about a women, Carolyn McKinstry, who had been inside The 16th Street Baptist Church in Birmingham, Alabama that had been bombed during the civil rights movement. She talked about how she felt guilty her whole life because she didn't do anything to prevent the bombing. Why had she survived when her friends had not? Well of course that sounds silly; how would a 12-year-old girl have known what was about to happen? How could she have prevented other children from dying? It was truly a wrong time, right place for her and a wrong time, wrong place for her friends. (If you want to explore this further, read her book *While the World Watched*. It's a fascinating first-hand account of that time in our country's history that you likely won't find in history books.)

Somehow, as I sat there listening to her tell her story, something came over me that just clicked. I needed to put the past behind me and remember the lessons I had learned. To not carry around constant thoughts of what I should have done, could have done, would have done if my thinking had been different. I did the best I knew how at the time. Just like my husband had been doing all along.

When I think about where I wanted to be after 20 years of marriage, it certainly wasn't as a single woman, watching others be happy couples planning life together, bearing the full financial responsibility of raising a daughter, and wondering how many years I had left all on my own.

And I hear what those gals are saying is the plus side of living alone: I get to eat what I want when I want, come and go as I please, spend my money however I choose, watch anything I like on TV, sing as loud as I want in the car, take long bubble baths in silence, read a book all night, and pretty much anything I like. But what I have realized is that I could have done all those things as a wife, too. And if these other women would take a step back and look at their lives, they would realize they can, too. Unfortunately, I just wasn't married to someone who thought those things were alright to do.

Honestly, the grass is not greener on the other side of the fence. But sometimes you have to climb the fence anyway.

"Love the Lord your God with all you heart and with all your soul and with all your mind. ...And love your neighbor as yourself."

Matthew 22:37-39 (NIV)

Chapter Four

For the Love of Friends

Shaking my head at the thought of all Carolee had gone through, she told me it could always be worse. Once again, she surprised me with another story or two to show me the truth behind this statement.

"My mother-in-law has stage four cancer!"

You could have knocked me over with a feather when I heard those words from a close friend. This woman was a vibrant, self-sufficient, strong-willed person. Unfortunately, she was also very cold to her family.

The fact she would not allow anyone to provide any care to her during this crisis led to a long discussion of how to care for someone you're not close to, even though you want to be. The anxiety of the person trying to help and the stress of the person experiencing the trauma will often cause additional stress for everyone involved! My advice was to just wait until she said what she needed. Trying to push yourself and your own ideas of help can often make the situation worse.

"But," I told my friend, "What you can do is pray."

When I was recovering in the hospital, I was talking with one of the nurses on duty about the power of prayer. She told me she had read about a study once where the researchers were trying to determine if prayer in fact made a difference in patient's recovery. She claimed they found that it did. Even in patients who had no faith or those being prayed for by complete strangers.

(I looked for this study myself but could find no conclusive evidence.)

It's interesting the people who come along with no personal experience of your circumstances, but who try to convince you they know best how you should handle it!

I received many books when I was in the hospital, but I really did not feel like reading about the best ways to handle cancer, survive cancer, keep cancer from returning, and so on! Several months following my last treatment, I decided to donate the books. But I thought I should also at least take a look through them out of respect for those who were only trying to help in giving them to me in the first place. One such book addressed proper nutrition for cancer patients. However, it did not address my type of cancer. It was an interesting story about a doctor who had recovered from brain cancer twice. Honestly, it simply came down to common sense eating habits that we all know are what we should do, cancer or not! More fruits and vegetables, avoid processed food and sugars, etc. Also, avoid stressful situations and surround yourself with positive people.

I decided to give this particular book to a relative who was the caregiver to a long-time friend dying from cancer. She was determined to read anything she could that might help her friend. Then I made the mistake of telling my friend who gave me the book as a gift that I had passed it along. She was very upset and could not understand my action. She demanded to know, "How could you give that away? It's so important! I will get you another copy."

Taking a breath and feeling terrible, I found the courage to say, "I am so sorry. I wanted someone else to find some comfort in it. But I no longer have cancer. It's very stressful to me to have books around that remind me of nothing but cancer."

It was one of the most difficult things I have ever said to someone I love. Especially to someone with nothing but good intentions in their heart. But sometimes you just have to put your foot down when you're in a situation that cannot be understood by someone else. Especially a situation you never want anyone to ever understand.

The ironic part about this is that a couple of years later, I did the exact same thing myself! My adorable grandson has a chronic illness. He is a darling little boy, but I have never known anyone with this illness. I was reading an inspirational magazine one day and there was a story of a little boy with the same condition as my grandson who grew up and found a way to turn his favorite activity into a successful career in music. Looking for a way to inspire my daughter and son-in-law with hope, I promptly shared the story, telling them that their son has so many great interests, they could likely help him in the same way. My ever patient son-in-law simply sighed and said, “Well, every case is different.”

How quickly we forget the lessons we have learned! This is one I will never forget.

Remember the business card I had found on day three in the hospital? Well, over the long days that dragged into the even longer, darker nights that month, I looked at that card often and just held on to the promise in the message it contained of *trusting in God*. Somewhere along the line though, I lost that card. To this day I’ve never been able to find it again. We have come to comment when situations like this happen as “chalk it up to the Lost Fairy.”

A reminder of the Lost Fairy came several years later when a beautiful woman from church was dying from cancer. This gentle lady of faith was in her early 70s, a wife married to her high school sweetheart for 50 years and was dying from stomach cancer. She called out of the blue one day to tell me about her cross.

You see, I still had that cross my friend Rose had given me that Sunday morning when she visited early in my treatments. I would cling to that small wooden cross often. Many nights I slept with it and awakened in the morning gripping tightly onto its promises.

After my weeks in the hospital, I started a practice of sending small hand-held crosses to people in need. They were made by women in Bethlehem from their local olive trees. Not every situation would deem this gift, but in times of crisis or uncertainty I would feel God whispering, *“They need one of My crosses. Send the love of Jesus to them.”*

Cheryl from church was one of these people. I had given a cross to her when she was first diagnosed, and I'd been praying for her for months. One Thursday, she called to tell me about her cross. I listened in wonderment as she described something that had happened to her that week.

She said she had to go to the emergency room because she was bleeding profusely. She put the cross (which she called "your cross") on her bedside table at home because she said she did not want it to get lost in the hustle and bustle of the emergency room at the hospital. When she got home a couple of days later, she asked her husband, "Where is Carolee's cross?" Her loving husband looked everywhere, turning the bedroom upside down, most of the house actually, and even the backyard wondering if the dog had somehow taken it outside.

Cheryl was heartbroken her cross was gone. "Because," she continued to tell me, "That cross has given me so much peace and hope." Just the same as it had done for me. "Cheryl," I said, "I'm sorry. I can get you another one." But she interrupted me and exclaimed, "Oh no! That's not where my story ends!" Cheryl went on to explain she finally fell sleep praying to God, "Please bring Carolee's cross back to me and give me that peace once again."

Holding my breath, I asked, "OK then what happened?" She said, "This morning I woke up and there it sat on my bedside table just where I had left it a few days earlier. I asked my husband where he had found my cross. The best part of this story is he swears he didn't find it at all. He said it wasn't there when he went to bed last night either." Cheryl went on to tell me that she felt she had to tell me this story before she left all of us.

She explained further, *"You and your faith have given me the hope and the peace with this little cross as a reminder that even when I leave my husband, my family and my friends on this earth and go home to heaven, everyone will be fine and I will see Jesus."*

We chatted a few more minutes and honestly I don't have any idea what else was said. I stopped listening as I contemplated what she had just told me. But I did know it was likely the last time I would talk with Cheryl on this side of heaven. And it was. The thing that really meant so much to me was the beautiful eulogy her husband gave as a tribute to their love during her funeral service the next month. Following the service I was talking with Cheryl's daughter and asked her if she had heard the story about the cross?

This young mother took my hand, smiled and said, "My mother spent the last days she was able to talk telling people that story. That beautiful story of God's love." At this point she paused and looked deep in my eyes. With tears in her eyes, she continued, "We buried your cross with my mother."

"For I know the plans I have for you," declares the Lord, "plans to prosper you and not to harm you, plans to give you hope and a future."

Jeremiah 29:11 (NIV)

Chapter Five

Always Looking Forward

I would imagine at this point you might be wondering how it was that I came to meet Carolee and that she would take so long to share her story with me. It's because we spent many a day in the outpatient chemotherapy floor at the same hospital where she had lived those 35 days. I too am a cancer survivor. And the lessons Carolee shared are so similar to my own. Through the years that followed I have met many cancer survivors who will share their own God-whispers. They're not all the same, but we have a common knowledge among us. One where we understand life is very short. Small things really do not matter. Money does not buy happiness. Find the people in your life who mean the most and embrace them. Weed out those who do not add joy to your life. Love your family with all your heart. We should get to know people really well. Be there for them; drop what you are doing and go when those people call.

And above all, when someone asks you to pray, do so with every ounce of your being.

During all the time I sat and listened to Carolee, I could not help but think about my own life. I'm very blessed to be married to a wonderful man I met years ago. Our love came from a long ago friendship. We have experienced such a good life. We travelled and explored not only the beauty of mountain peaks, the roar of waves in the pacific northwest, and sandy beaches of the southern most point of the United States, but more importantly, we experienced a love that some people spend their whole lives searching for. A mutual respect and admiration for each other has made for the best marriage possible. When I was diagnosed with cancer, my husband was with me every step of the way, holding my hand, at times so tightly that I could literally feel his pulse and know he wished he could take it all away.

My love asked me one time why I wouldn't let him come with me for these follow-up infusions. Well, anyone who has gone through this knows it's just plain boring. Hours and hours with nothing to do except watch the clock tick the hours away. Sure, you can read or sleep, but either is not much fun for a companion to experience. Plus, I was really just being selfish. As the weeks passed by, I could not wait to get there and listen to more of Carolee's story. I wanted to learn the lessons for myself which she had shared so openly with me.

Eventually, my treatments ended. By the grace of God, both Carolee and I experienced a full recovery. As anyone knows, cancer doesn't really end there. You wait and you watch and you wonder if and when and how it will return. Eventually with time, those worries do tend to fade. Learning the many lessons gleaned from the entire experience and how to put them to use helps. I thought I would share a few of the things I did to get past my own diagnosis and continued fears. Some of these were suggestions from Carolee. Some we did together. Some I learned to find and follow through on my own.

I had my own Esther moment a while ago. I was watching television one night and the thoughts of a cancer return started creeping in. I happened to be watching a rerun of an old favorite, *The Waltons*. As I watched the story unfold, I realized one of the teenagers in the story was Ron Howard (Opie from the old *Andy Griffith* television series). And you guessed it, he was diagnosed with leukemia! Of course during the Great Depression, the era of *The Waltons*, there was no cure at all for this disease, so he knew he was dying. As I continued to watch, I started thinking about this large fictional family and naming each of the characters as they appeared on screen. But I could not remember a time during all the seasons I had watched this show when they called the grandmother by her first name. At that very moment, God whispered to me, *listen*. And the grandfather on the show called out to his wife, "Esther!"

And I knew for certain that I had nothing to worry about.

I attend a wonderful Bible study at times. I listen to a lot of people talk about how they get by in life. I read daily devotions every morning. I have a very diverse group of ten friends who get together every few months so we can contemplate how best to love others. I meditate and pray. I write in a gratitude journal every few days (I try to do it daily, but that doesn't always happen).

Why do I do all of these things? Because there is never a time when we shouldn't be trying to figure out how to be our best self. If we are not working toward that, then there really is no point in being around other people.

So taking that into consideration, let me share a few other things that I do based on words of wisdom from some wonderful friends. One of the best pieces of advice I ever heard was to stop trying to get your entire "To Do" list done. It's just not possible. For everything you accomplish, something else will always need to be done. Learn how to be okay with that! Life is just too busy and stressful, no matter your situation and no matter how hard you try to make it not.

So what do you do when life gets entirely too out of focus with responsibilities? Do this. Write down the top three compliments you ever received. And it can't be, "that's a pretty dress." Or, "you look handsome." Make them something very personal that really made a difference when you heard it.

My top one is, "You are the strongest person I know."

Not literally. But I have heard this from multiple people through the years. Likely because of how I handled (often times) situations that I actually brought about myself from bad choices! But, if we can come out on the other side a better person, it's worth the trouble. That's why this is my top compliment.

Search your memory. Find some that make you feel good about yourself. Write them down and keep them with you. Then look at them often.

The other thing I like to do is find three focus words at the start of every year. They can have multiple meanings. Think about this, too. What words motivate you? Here are some of mine: strength (yes, to lift heavy objects, but also to keep my mind strong, be a shoulder for others to lean on, etc.), patience (in waiting on God's perfect timing instead of my own, in waiting on others, in meeting goals, etc.), and endurance (keep moving forward, stay the course, etc.). Again, carry these with you. When life starts spiraling out of control, take a look at them and think about why you wrote them down in the first place. I guarantee you will re-focus your thoughts and actions if you do.

Speaking of goals, what are yours? Do you have any? Do you know? I really believe that if I'm not working on something long term, then I am just spinning my wheels. And not to say we shouldn't live in the moment. That is something I have really been working on the last couple of years. I often get so busy with social and work obligations, that I find myself always looking ahead to the next thing I had to be ready for instead of enjoying what was happening right that very moment. Not to mention the people who were right there. How quickly we can forget previous thoughts. Remember when one of the lessons Carolee learned from being sick was that she felt she knew a lot of people, but didn't know many people very well? Honestly! I had to re-set that lesson and start paying attention. Now! Love the people right in front of me!

The last thing I would say is that I do my best to not live in a "what if?" world. Think about this, too. I absolutely adore Beth Moore Bible studies (thank you, Carolee). She is a delight who can describe a scene from Biblical days that will bring tears to your eyes, all while telling a story about her own life that will make you laugh till you cry! One of my favorite stories she told was on this exact subject. She said, (and I'm paraphrasing because I watched this video a long time ago) "OK. What is the very worst thing that could ever happen to you? Think about it. If you're a believer, the answer is not dying. So what could it be here on this earth?" She goes on to tell what her worst thing would be, but the point is, she then asks, "So what if that actually happened? Then what? And then what?" Keep asking until you are face down on the floor crying out to God for mercy. Well, I haven't gone there, but you get the idea. What is the actual point in worrying about something that likely will never happen? Because really, the what-if's are really just our unspoken fears. I read a quote somewhere that said "fear is temporary atheism." That has always stuck with me.

I learned a long time ago, God hasn't left me yet. Why would He now?

One of my very best friends sums up our view of ourselves in this way. Ask yourself, "What are three words that best describe me?" Do you know? Mine have always been "I'm a peacemaker." It actually goes hand in hand with "What's your purpose?" But it also goes a bit deeper, as it really makes you analyze what you're all about in general. Try it. Take a minute and just think. It's worth the time. I promise.

So what's next? What's on my bucket list? As I said, I have a wonderful life full of love. So, I asked Carolee what was on her bucket list? Here's what she said...

I prayed for a beautiful bright home full of peace and joy and calm. I waited patiently and God brought it to me. I prayed for the return to perfect health in mind, body, and spirit. I waited the five years it took and God gave it to me. I asked for financial security, for my divorce to be final, for my daughters to be happy and healthy. And God gave them all to me.

The prayer that Jabez prayed in the Bible reads in part, "Bless me and expand my territory." (I Chronicles 4:10, NIV)

Now, I pray for a house with a little yard that I can own and call my own. One where I can put my feet in the grass and drink my coffee and listen to the birds and feel never ending gratitude to God for all the mercy He has shown me in this lifetime. I have a list in my prayer journal of all the many features I would like in my home, but at the top of the list beyond a comfortable living room and front porch, high ceilings and a farmer's sink in the kitchen are the words bright, joyful, inviting, safe, and peaceful.

And of course, I pray for love, true love. Not a love with someone I think I need. But to wait for the true love that God wanted for me all along. That's another page in my prayer journal. And yes there are words including tall and attractive, financially stable with good manners, etc. But more importantly at the top of that list are the words faith-filled, considerate, honest, grateful, and joyful. And I know if I can be all of those things, then I can wait patiently for God to bring this to me, too. His blessings are never ending when we just ask, wait, and live in His grace.

And guess what? It took me many years to tell anyone my story. I kept putting it off. So many people asked me, "What are you waiting for? Your story is one of hope even in the worst of circumstances." People with cancer have come and gone, some have survived and some have not. And with every diagnosis, I have told myself, "I guess I should tell my story to someone. People need it!"

"Because," Carolee went on to explain, "My favorite stories are not those that tell about cancer, but those that bring hope. The stories of people who make us laugh and cry and make us think about what's really important."

This is Carolee's ending.

I did wait patiently in my last hope for a life filled with someone all my own to love. To spend my senior years with. To grow old with, enjoying our children and grandchildren. Someone to smile with, laugh with, hold hands with, and love. And just like the saying goes, it happened when I least expected it. Seemingly out of nowhere, an old friendship appeared and rekindled. It happened slowly, over many months of talking, of silence, of texts, of broken plans, and finally many long telephone conversations. But it happened most of all because of honesty. Sharing life's most fragile memories with someone turned into an appreciation of all this life offers when we trust in another. When we finally took time to be together in person, *it was God who whispered, "I am here and this is for you."*

At one point, we had a discussion about our differences in personalities and he said to me, "Sometimes, I think you picked the wrong guy." From seemingly nowhere, I replied, "I didn't pick you, God did." I will never forget his response, "Well, OK then." And that is how we live our relationship. Praying that God is with us, leading our every step into our future together. I never want to love again without God leading the way.

WORDS OF THE DAY

You may recall from earlier in Carolee's story that her parents had finally divorced. One of my favorite stories she told was how her dad had met her stepmom.

He was attending a conference in Atlanta as a getaway with friends. The next time he met Carolee for dinner following his return, he explained that he needed her advice. He had met this lovely woman on the trip and they had connected in a way he had never before connected with another woman.

He was 53 years old at that time. Carolee wanted to know what advice she could possibly offer. Carolee's dad said the problem was that he didn't know how to get in touch with her. You have to realize this was before cell phones, the internet, Google, etc., which seems unbelievable since now we can find anyone, anywhere, anytime with these tools! Also, he wasn't sure if he should try to find her because he had just recently finalized his divorce with her mother.

Carolee said, "My advice then (and would still be now) was that there is no time like the present to go for happiness. And, if she made him happy, then he should definitely try to find her and see where things led." Then she made the profound statement, "Besides, you don't have to marry her!"

So he contacted a friend who knew her and he did in fact reconnect with her. Not only was it meant to be, but a year later they actually did marry and they have remained married for the past 30 years!

Carolee went on to tell me that she knew this was one of the best things that ever happened to not only her dad, but to her as well. Sarah became one of her very favorite "Esthers." The love Carolee had in her eyes as she talked about her stepmom was apparent. She continued, "I do not know what kind of a person I would be today had she not entered my life as an adult. She has definitely taught me how to be a better daughter, even though she never had any biological children of her own. Her example guided me to become a stepmother that I can say I have been proud to be to Kate. In all the years since, Sarah has not only been my stepmother, friend, and confidant, she has become my Mama."

Never having a stepmother, nor being a stepmother, this was hard for me to grasp. But Carolee continued.

When I became sick, she was heartbroken. She would tell me, "Your Dad is so strong in his faith and remains very quietly in prayer. I try to as well, but I can't stop crying at the thought of losing my girl!" As only a mother knows, these words ring true at the thought of any crisis happening to her child.

I have often reminded my Mama that regardless of her own feelings, she never once stopped putting me first. Every day for 30 of the 35 days

I was confined to my hospital room, she would text me a word or two of encouragement, based on what was happening that day.

Sarah's words of the day:

You are filled with grace.

A loving heart.

Faith filled.

Strong.

Enveloped in love.

Cherished.

In God's shining light.

A gift to me.

Watched over by angels.

Blast free!!!

Awesome!

Amazing.

In my heart.

Overflowing with peace, love and platelets.

Wrapped in God's love (and of all your family and friends).

Patience, perseverance and optimism.

Warmed by the love of God, family, and friends.

So special to so many.

Our love to keep you warm.

A blessing to all who know and love you.

Lifted up by so very many.

Patience and perseverance.

Inspiring to all who know and love you… Any doubts about that?

Dazzling - beautiful in heart and soul.

Gracious.

Patience.

Getting so close.

Hoping and praying with you!

Yea!!!!

Dancin'!!!

VERSES OF HOPE

Some time after our recovery, I had just finished taking a yoga class with Carolee. As we left the studio, she stopped me and pulled several sheets of paper from her bag. Handing them to me, she explained.

My Esther story began when I was born. But it truly came to light when I was diagnosed with cancer. Over the next several years, I received countless texts, emails, and cards, all filled with inspiration and messages of hope. I began to document the Bible verses written within the cards early during my hospital stay. By the time the cards stopped arriving many months later, I had accumulated a total of 217. These are the Bible verses contained within many of them. It was interesting to see how many were used in various forms and from different versions of *The Bible,* as you will read here. They brought me hope at a time I needed it most, as they continue to do today. These verses are a copy for you. (The Bible NIV)

2 Chronicles 20: "We are the army of The Lord and the battle is His."

2 Corinthians 1:3-4 "Praise be to God and Father of our Lord Jesus Christ, the Father of compassion and the God of all comfort, Who comforts us in all our troubles..."

2 Corinthians 12:8-10 "Three times I pleaded with the Lord to take it away from me. But he said to me, "My grace is sufficient for you, for my power is made perfect in weakness." Therefore I will boast all the more gladly about my weaknesses, so that Christ's power may rest on me. That is why, for Christ's sake, I delight in weaknesses, in insults, in hardships, in persecutions, in difficulties. For when I am weak, then I am strong."

2 Corinthians 13:14 "May the grace of the Lord Jesus Christ, and the love of God, and the fellowship of the Holy Spirit be with you all."

Ecclesiastes 3 "To everything there is a season..."

Exodus 15:26 "I am The Lord, Who heals you."

Hebrews 11:1 "Faith is being sure of what we hope for and certain of what we do not see."

Hebrews 12:1 "Let us run with endurance the race that is set before us."

Isaiah 41:10 "I am your God. I will strengthen you and help you. I will uphold you with My righteous right hand."

&

"Do not fear, for I am with you; Do not anxiously look about you, for I am your God. I will strengthen you...I will uphold you.

&

"So do not fear, for I am with you; do not be dismayed, for I am your God. I will strengthen you and help you; I will uphold you with my righteous right hand."

Isaiah 33:2 “O Lord, be gracious to us... Be our strength every morning.”

Isaiah 40:31 “but those who hope in the Lord will renew their strength. They will soar on wings like eagles; they will run and not grow weary, they will walk and not be faint.”

Isaiah 49:15-16 “I will not forget you! See, I have engraved you on the palms of my hands.”

Jeremiah 29:11 “For I know the plans I have for you,” declares the Lord, “plans to prosper you and not to harm you, plans to give you hope and a future.”

1 John 4:7 “Beloved, let us love one another; for love is of God.”

John 10:10 “I came that they may have life, and have it abundantly.”

Joshua 1:9 “Have I not commanded you? Be strong and courageous. Do not be afraid; do not be discouraged, for the Lord your God will be with you wherever you go.”

Lamentations 3:22-23 “The Lord's love never ends; His mercies never stop. They are new every morning.”

Luke 9:57 “As they were walking along the road, a man said to him, “I will follow you wherever you go.”

Luke 17:19 “Then He said to him, “Rise and go; your faith has made you well.”

Mark 10:27 “All things are possible with God.”

Mark 11:24 “Whatever you ask for in prayer, believe that you have received it, and it will be yours.”

Matthew 6:30 “And if God cares so wonderfully for flowers that are here today and gone tomorrow, won’t He more surely care for you?”

Matthew 8:19 “Then a teacher of the law came to him and said, “Teacher, I will follow you wherever you go.”

Nehemiah 8:10 “The joy of the Lord is your strength.”

Numbers 6:24-25 “The Lord bless you and keep you; The Lord make his face shine upon you.”

1 Peter 5:10 “And the God of all grace...will Himself restore you and make you strong, firm and steadfast.”

Philippians 1:3 “I thank my God every time I remember you.”

Philippians 1:7 “You have a very special place in my heart.”

Philippians 2:13 “...for it is God who works in you to will and to act according to his good purpose.”

Philippians 4:4-9 “Rejoice in the Lord always. I will say it again: Rejoice! Let your gentleness be evident to all. The Lord is near. Do not be anxious about anything, but in every situation, by prayer and petition, with thanksgiving, present your requests to God. And the peace of God, which transcends all understanding, will guard your hearts and your minds in Christ Jesus. Finally, brothers and sisters, whatever is true, whatever is noble, whatever is right, whatever is pure, whatever is lovely, whatever is admirable—if anything is excellent or praiseworthy—think about such things. Whatever you have learned or received or heard from me, or seen in me—put it into practice. And the God of peace will be with you.”

Philippians 4:13 “I can do all things through Him who strengthens me.”

Philippians 4:19 "My God will use His wonderful riches in Christ Jesus to give you everything you need."

Proverbs 3

Wisdom Bestows Well-Being

1. My son, do not forget my teaching,
   but keep my commands in your heart,
2. for they will prolong your life many years
   and bring you peace and prosperity.
3. Let love and faithfulness never leave you;
   bind them around your neck,
   write them on the tablet of your heart.
4. Then you will win favor and a good name
   in the sight of God and man.
5. Trust in the Lord with all your heart
   and lean not on your own understanding;
6. in all your ways submit to him,
   and he will make your paths straight.[a]
7. Do not be wise in your own eyes;
   fear the Lord and shun evil.
8. This will bring health to your body
   and nourishment to your bones.
9. Honor the Lord with your wealth,
   with the first fruits of all your crops;
10. then your barns will be filled to overflowing,

and your vats will brim over with new wine.

11. My son, do not despise the Lord's discipline,

and do not resent his rebuke,

12. because the Lord disciplines those he loves,

as a father the son he delights in.[b]

13. Blessed are those who find wisdom,

those who gain understanding,

14. for she is more profitable than silver

and yields better returns than gold.

15. She is more precious than rubies;

nothing you desire can compare with her.

16. Long life is in her right hand;

in her left hand are riches and honor.

17. Her ways are pleasant ways,

and all her paths are peace.

18. She is a tree of life to those who take hold of her;

those who hold her fast will be blessed.

19. By wisdom the Lord laid the earth's foundations,

by understanding he set the heavens in place;

20. by his knowledge the watery depths were divided,

and the clouds let drop the dew.

21. My son, do not let wisdom and understanding out of your sight,

preserve sound judgment and discretion;

22. they will be life for you,

an ornament to grace your neck.

23. Then you will go on your way in safety,
    and your foot will not stumble.
24. When you lie down, you will not be afraid;
    when you lie down, your sleep will be sweet.
25. Have no fear of sudden disaster
    or of the ruin that overtakes the wicked,
26. for the Lord will be at your side
    and will keep your foot from being snared.

Psalm 16:1 “Keep me safe, my God for in you I take refuge.”

Psalm 16:5 “Lord, you alone are my portion and my cup; you make my lot secure.”

Psalm 16:8 “I keep my eyes always on the Lord. With him at my right hand, I will not be shaken.”

Psalm 18:29 “With your help, I can advance against a troop; with my God, I can scale a wall.”

Psalm 27:4 “This is what I seek: that I may dwell in the house of The Lord all the days of my life, to gaze upon the beauty of The Lord.”

Psalm 28:8 “The Lord is their strength...”

Psalm 29:11 “The Lord gives strength to His people; The Lord blesses His people with peace.”

Psalm 30:2 “O Lord my God, I called to You...and You healed me.”

Psalm 31:14-16 “But I trust in you o Lord; I say! ‘You are my God.’ My times are in your hands; deliver me from my enemies and from those who pursue me. Let your face shine on your servant. Save me in your unfailing love."

Psalm 33:5 "The earth is full of the goodness of the Lord."

Psalm 37:5 "Trust in Him."

Psalm 63:6-8 "On my bed I remember you;

I think of you through the watches of the night.

Because you are my help, I sing in the shadow of your wings.

My soul clings to you, your right hand upholds me."

Psalm 73:28 "But as for me, it is good to be near God."

Psalm 118:24 "This is the day The Lord hath made. Let us rejoice and be glad in it."

Psalm 138:3 "When I pray You answer me by giving me the strength I need."

Psalm 139

1. You have searched me, Lord,
   and you know me.
2. You know when I sit and when I rise;
   you perceive my thoughts from afar.
3. You discern my going out and my lying down;
   you are familiar with all my ways.
4. Before a word is on my tongue
   you, Lord, know it completely.
5. You hem me in behind and before,
   and you lay your hand upon me.

6. Such knowledge is too wonderful for me,
too lofty for me to attain.
7. Where can I go from your Spirit?
Where can I flee from your presence?
8. If I go up to the heavens, you are there;
if I make my bed in the depths, you are there.
9. If I rise on the wings of the dawn,
if I settle on the far side of the sea,
10. even there your hand will guide me,
your right hand will hold me fast.
11. If I say, "Surely the darkness will hide me
and the light become night around me,"
12. even the darkness will not be dark to you;
the night will shine like the day,
for darkness is as light to you.
13. For you created my inmost being;
you knit me together in my mother's womb.
14. I praise you because I am fearfully and wonderfully made;
your works are wonderful,
I know that full well.
15. My frame was not hidden from you
when I was made in the secret place,
when I was woven together in the depths of the earth.
16. Your eyes saw my unformed body;
all the days ordained for me were written in your book

before one of them came to be.

17. How precious to me are your thoughts,[a] God!

    How vast is the sum of them!

18. Were I to count them,

    they would outnumber the grains of sand—

    when I awake, I am still with you.

Romans 8:28 "In all things God works for the good of those who love Him."

Romans 8:39 "Neither height nor depth, nor anything else in all creation, will be able to separate us from the love of God that is in Christ Jesus our Lord."

Romans 15:13 "May the God of hope fill you with all joy and peace as you trust in him so that you may be filled with hope by the power of the Holy Spirit."

2 Timothy 4:22 "The Lord be with your spirit."

Zephaniah 3:17 "The Lord your God is with you...He will quiet you with His love..."

AUTHOR'S AFTERWORD

The story of Carolee and her companion listening to her was created from my imagination, but was drawn from my own experience with cancer; leukemia to be exact! I use the word experience because so often people use the word journey. A journey is something you choose to take. Cancer is definitely not something anyone would choose.

I talked in my first book, "Whatever Works for You" how much I dislike the statement "I don't have time for that!" Time becomes very different, as does normal, once you've gone through something like this. You really start thinking about what you are doing with the time you have here on this earth.

How many people do you know who just can never get things done, even though they would like to, but they continually use the justification they're disorganized, or they don't have time, or they have too many things pulling at them, or, or, or? Fill in the blank. I think each of us are at least a little bit like these people. There's always going to be something to distract us and take away our time. But are you going to let those distractions come between you and what you want? What you really want to do in this lifetime with the moments that you have left?

Stop trying to do it all!

It keeps you from doing anything. And truly look at your goals. Look at who you want to be. Look at who you want to be remembered as. Are those the things that you're doing now that will get you to that point in the end? Are you using your time that you have left to really make a difference, be the person you want to be, and live the life you want?

Truly, the biggest lesson that I've learned through all of my life experience is to have patience. To trust, to wait, to meditate, to pray, to be humble, and to be honest. Most of all to keep giving and giving to others. To set goals. To reach for those goals no matter how long they take. It took me 40 years to reach my very first goal and it's been another seven to reach the next ones. My to do list will be there, so I do my best to make it one that's worthwhile. Make it one that's memorable. Make it one that makes a difference for other people; one that brings them joy. Because at the end of the day, I have found that dreams can come true when you set aside trying to control everything and simply love others instead.

Shortly after I recovered from cancer, I was asked to speak about my experience to a room full of health care workers. I wanted once again to be able to provide hope while showing my appreciation for the many blessings provided to me. I had lots of notes written on 3x5 cards, so I wouldn't forget anything I wanted to say. While I was thumbing through them before my speech, a very faith-filled woman came over to me and asked what I was doing. I explained I needed to get this story "right."

And then I heard God whisper through her.

As she took both my hands and looked me in the eyes with pure love, she said, "You don't need those cards. *Just tell your story. Tell what's in your heart.*"

Once I was introduced, I took a deep breath, set the cards face down on the podium, looked out into the room and just started talking. I finished by saying, "Thank you. Thank you for the work you do every day to help total strangers. Strangers just like me."

Imagine my surprise when the administrator of the number one hospital in the region came up to me after and gave me a hug! He looked at me with a huge smile and said, "Thank you. That was just what I needed to hear this morning."

So this is my prayer for you. That you will take the time to tell your story. Just write it down. Tell it to your children. Tell it to your best friend. Write it down and read it to yourself. Look back over your life through the words that is your story to tell. It's important. You are important. The world needs to know who you are. You just never know what good you have to offer until you take that first step to give back, reach out, tell your story, and thank God.

Because life is always surprising. Sometimes the things you think are going to happen don't happen at all. Sometimes the things you think will never happen do. And sometimes miracles happen.

Keep listening. God is whispering to you, too.

FINAL THOUGHTS

I'm leaving you with one last "Thank You!" When I was 19 years old, someone came into my life who left a profound appreciation of the word friendship in me to this very day. His name is Larry Allen and he has graciously edited both of my books. My first non-fiction book and now this fictional story. When I was diagnosed with cancer, he was one of the people who continually stayed in touch, always with a thought to make me laugh, as he has done throughout the years. As I said earlier about Carolee's story, I drew much of the detail from my own experience with leukemia, even using the same timeframe of the holidays and months after to tell her story. One year after my remission, Larry sent me the following email. I have cherished his words ever since, as I have each day of our friendship. I am grateful for his permission to share this note.

December 25th – Day Three Hundred Seventy-Eight: Christmas and me...and you

Happy Merry!

I'm home from church, everything's done, and I'm getting ready to call it a night (It's 12:15 a.m. Christmas morning as I write this...) I just thought I'd drop you a little holiday message before I went to sleep. I want to share a few thoughts with you this Christmas night, because sharing with you is important.

I wanted to tell you how the last year of your life has changed mine. Much of it you already know, I imagine, but humor me while I type out what's inside my brain.

Last December, when I first received the text message sharing your illness with me and your other friends, I was sitting alone at a Wendy's eating lunch. I kept reading it over and over, thinking there was something I was missing or something that I didn't understand. There was no way you had leukemia--it simply wasn't possible.

In those first moments, something very fundamental shifted inside me. The reality of the uncertainty of the future hit me solidly in the head. More than at any other time in my life, I came to terms with the fact that tomorrow is promised to no one, and that it is incredibly important we "say and do" while we can, because none of us knows when that ability may be taken away, for whatever reason.

I look at things much differently now than I did 12 months ago. Guys my age fall over dead all the time (sigh...). I think about what I would want you to know if I never had the chance to talk to you again.

Next week you celebrate your first year of good news. What a great Christmas present! And it is a great present to share with those of us who care about you. But the first gift that I received when all this began was the gift of "living in the moment." Thanks to you, your experiences, and your responses, I will never assume the safety of the future. I will tell the people in my life what they need to know from me now and share what God has placed in my heart. Whatever good may come from that comes from you.

And what would I share today? That you have changed me forever. That I hope your life remains blessed with good things. And that I will always be your greatest admirer.

Merry Christmas,

Larry

RECOMMENDED READING

"365 Thank Yous" by John Kralik

"Jesus the One and Only" by Beth Moore

"Love Does" by Bob Goff

"The Dash" by Linda Ellis

"The Go-Giver" by Bob Burg

"The Noticer" by Andy Andrews

"The Prayer of Jabez" by Bruce Wilkinson

"The Purpose Driven Life" by Rick Warren

"Whatever Works for You" by Deborah McVay-McKinney

"While the World Watched" by Carolyn McKinstry

"Women's Devotional Bible" (NIV) by Zondervan Publishing House

"Guideposts" monthly magazine and "Daily Guideposts" daily devotion by www.Guideposts.org

"I AM"

I am a child of God. (Romans 8:16)

I am forgiven. (Colossians 1:13,14)

I am saved by grace through faith. (Ephesians 2:8)

I am justified (Romans 5:1)

I am sanctified (1 Corinthians 6:11)

I am a new creature. (2 Corinthians 5:17)

I am kept in safety wherever I go (Psalms 91:11)

I am strong in the Lord & in the power of His might (Ephesians 6:10)

I am doing all things through Christ who strengthens me (Philippians 4:13)

I am an heir of God and a joint heir with Jesus (Romans 8:17)

I am blessed coming in & going out (Deuteronomy 28:6)

I am an heir to eternal life (1 John 5:11,12)

I am healed by His strips (1 Peter 2:24)

I am more than a conqueror (Romans 8:37)

I am bringing every thought into captivity (2 Corinthians 10:5)

I am being transformed by renewing my mind (Romans 12:1,2)

I am the light of the world (Matthew 5:14)

I am fearfully & wonderfully made. (Psalm 139:14)

Biblegateway.com

Printed in the United States
By Bookmasters